Independent Living

Also by the author:

Turing Test

Magic Test

Meghan's Dragon

Date Night on Union Station

Alien Night on Union Station

High Priest on Union Station

Spy Night on Union Station

Carnival on Union Station

Wanderers on Union Station

Vacation on Union Station

Guest Night on Union Station

Word Night on Union Station

Party Night on Union Station

Review Night on Union Station

Family Night on Union Station

Book Night on Union Station

LARP Night on Union Station

Career Night on Union Station

Independent Living

EarthCent Circuit Ship

Foner Books

ISBN 978-1-948691-19-2

Northampton, Massachusetts

One

"You call this fish chowder?" Harry demanded indignantly. "It's last night's scrod special mashed up with milk."

"Next, please," the serving robot intoned in a mechanical voice. "One entrée per customer."

"Forget it, Harry," Irene told her husband. "It's just a bot, not artificial intelligence. You won't get any satisfaction there."

"As soon as we finish this so-called lunch, I'm going to track down Ms. Jane Hasslewraith and get our money back."

"We've only been here one night and we skipped breakfast to finish the leftovers from the meals we bought on the space elevator. Give it some time."

"If the food is this bad already, imagine what it will be like after we leave Earth orbit. Where's the cook going to find scrod in space?"

"You don't even like fish," his wife pointed out as she slid her tray along the cafeteria counter behind his. "Why didn't you take something else?"

"If you didn't notice, the other options were grilled cheese sandwiches that looked like they were made last month, and peanut butter and jelly with purple goo seeping through the white bread. The brochure claimed there would be a team of nutritionists working up custom diets for us!"

"It is independent living, after all, not a nursing home. Jane was very specific about that when we signed the contracts. And she said we could expect things to be a bit rocky until the ship leaves orbit because the staff are all vacationing on Earth and they'll take the last space elevator capsule up."

"Just look at this coffee," Harry complained. "It's so weak that I can see the bottom of the cup. If it wasn't for that giant display panel behind the counter showing the ship, I'd think I was in a prison cafeteria."

"Things can only get better. Why don't you go find us a couple of seats together while I make myself a cup of tea." Irene started rummaging through a cardboard box of individual tea bags that looked like they'd been purchased at an odd-lots store. "Maybe some of these people have been here a few days so they'll know more about what's going on than we do."

"The place is three-quarters empty," Harry muttered, but he took her advice and found a table with just two open seats to maximize the chance of learning something from the other residents. "Does anybody mind if my wife and I join you?"

"Is she invisible?" asked a bald man wearing a vest and bowtie who looked to be in his mid-seventies. A hand-printed sticker over the breast pocket of his shirt identified him as Dave.

"Irene is making herself a cup of tea," Harry explained, setting down his tray and pulling back both of the unoccupied chairs. "Hey, where did you get those club sandwiches?"

"You have to ask the bot," a tiny woman labeled Nancy told him. "It can't hold a conversation unless the ship's AI takes over, but it makes sandwiches to order if you ask."

"Hello, everybody," Irene said, placing her own tray on the table and bobbing her head at Harry as he slid in the chair as she sat. "Oh, were we supposed to have name tags? Nobody told us."

"There used to be a stack of them at the end of the cafeteria line, but they ran out two days ago and the bots don't know where to get more," Nancy told her. "You can make your own from paper and pin them on until you get to know everybody. I have pins if you need them."

Harry dipped his spoon in the fish chowder, raised it, and then let it fall in disgust. "Hey, did anybody else get woken up by a loud recording this morning? Something about calisthenics?"

"Every morning, and it's not a recording, it's the ship's AI," replied a fit-looking man whose sticker identified him as Jack. "She lets you slide your first day on board, but if you don't get out of bed and into the corridor tomorrow morning, she'll run the temperature in your room down to freezing, strobe the lights, and play this horrible whistling through the speakers."

"Dollnick opera," the tiny woman told them. "And the AI's name is Flower, the same as the ship."

"Which ones are the Dollnicks again?" Harry asked, pushing aside his chowder.

"You going to leave that?" Dave asked, eyeing the bowl.

"It's all yours."

"The Dollnicks are one of the intermediate space-faring species that breathe an oxygen-nitrogen mix," Nancy explained. "They've had faster-than-light technology for millions of years." She noted the lack of comprehension on

Harry's face and added, "They're the tall ones with four arms and feathered crests."

"Oh, right. So why would the ship's AI play their music in our apartments?"

"To get your lazy bones out of bed," Jack told them. "This is a Dollnick ship, after all, and Flower is a Dollnick AI. She probably likes their music."

"What do you mean we're on an alien ship? The saleslady promised us that the independent living facility is one hundred percent human owned."

"Actually, I'd feel better about my investment if this place was being run by the Dollnicks. I was a contract worker on two of their ag worlds, twenty years on the first and twenty-five years on the second. I would have signed up for another hitch to finish out my life, but they have rules about that."

"It's their version of mandatory retirement," Nancy told the others. "The Dollnicks have actuarial tables for all of the species they employ and they won't let you work full-time past eighty percent of your life expectancy."

"Don't want to get stuck paying for medical problems, I'll bet," Harry said.

"They're not like that," Jack insisted, his obvious sincerity coming through. "Respecting the elderly is a cultural thing with them. With all of the aliens I've come across."

"Well, Harry and I have never been off of Earth before, which is the main reason I let him talk me into giving this independent living place a try," Irene said. "We had to sell our home to come up with the deposit and it's not easy finding buyers in small towns these days. We were lucky that a young couple who worked for us were interested in taking over our bakery, so we sold them the whole building, along with our apartment upstairs."

"You were bakers?" the bald man asked eagerly. "I've been on board for two weeks now and the food in this cafeteria wasn't any better when I arrived. Maybe the two of you…"

"We're retired," Harry said forcefully, leaving no room for misinterpretation. "What did you do back on Earth?"

"Salesman," he replied, wiping out the now-empty chowder bowl with a slice of flimsy white bread. "I signed up for this independent living in space thing because of the startup discount. They say that people who wait for Flower's next visit to Earth will have to pay twice as much to buy into the complex."

"That was the main motivation for me as well," Nancy said. "I suppose there's a risk involved in anything new, but I never could have afforded it if I waited."

"I just wanted to get off of Earth, it was depressing going back there after forty-five years," Jack said. "I felt like a salmon returning home to die without the bonus of breeding. I didn't know anybody on Earth or own a home there, so I started looking into independent living places, just so I wouldn't be alone. This one place I actually visited was only three hundred creds a month for rent, but you had to take at least one meal a day."

"What did that cost?" Irene asked.

"A thousand creds a month." He laughed. "I could have rented an apartment on a Stryx station and ordered a takeout meal a day for that, with change left over."

"It was the same with the places near me," Nancy confirmed. "Some made you buy the unit you lived in, some rented, but all of them included a minimum of one meal a day whether you ate it or not. This place doesn't even start charging for meals until Flower leaves the solar system. After that, it's optional whether we eat here or at the main food court, and there must be hundreds of restaurants on board."

"Excuse me, but what day is it?" the bald man asked.

"It's Tuesday, Dave," Nancy informed him. "Do you have a date?"

"In addition to the morning calisthenics, Flower insists that everybody on board take up a team sport, but she makes an exception for health issues. She told me this morning that I have to go see the ship's physician after lunch."

"The ship's AI talks to us?" Irene asked.

"More than some of us would like," a woman without a nametag whispered.

"If she can hear us at this table, whispering won't change that," Nancy said. "The Dollnicks used voice commands for everything—well, whistling commands, in their case. There are speakers and microphones embedded throughout the ship, though you can find dead spots in large rooms like this when there are a number of conversations going on."

"What if the cafeteria were empty?" Irene asked.

"In that case, Flower will certainly hear if you speak clearly, but that doesn't mean she'll always answer. She's a bit eccentric."

"So why do you need to know the day if you already knew about the appointment, Dave?" Harry asked.

"Haven't you ever been to a doctor? That's the first thing they ask after you hit seventy. If you say you don't remember or get the day wrong, they start running tests to see if you're losing your mind."

"Our doctor on Earth always asked Harry if he remembered his name," Irene contributed, drawing an annoyed look from her husband.

"The doctor's name or his own?" Dave asked.

"My own," Harry grumbled. "He had a weird sense of humor."

"Well, I'm set for that as long as I'm wearing this name-tag, and I memorized where I live the first day I was on board. Deck 17, Corridor 3, Suite 62."

"You're two doors down from us," Irene observed.

"What do I need to remember all of that for?" Harry asked. "The saleslady said that the ship has smart lifts that will take you wherever you ask."

"And our home address is now Deck 17, Corridor 3, Suite 64," his wife told him. "Surely you don't expect the lift to remember where you live."

"What's wrong with saying, Shady Elms Independent Living?"

"Is that who you signed up with?" Nancy asked. "I'm with Shady Oaks."

"Shady Pines," Jack contributed.

"I'm Shady Elms too," Dave said. "That's probably why our cabins are so close together. I came up on the first elevator capsule when the ship arrived at Earth and I must have eaten at least one meal with everybody. We're all in Shady-something or another. I think the individual sales reps on Earth work as independent contractors for tax reasons."

"That makes sense," Harry allowed. "We had the same attorney who did the closing for our building go over the contract for this place and he said it was all pretty standard. I just wish we could have gotten in without the big deposit, but it's a money-back guarantee."

"That's what convinced me," Nancy said. "I lived in an apartment so I had to cash in part of my annuity to pay the key money. I used to be a teacher," she added, "but with so many parents keeping their children home to study with the free teacher bots, I could barely pay my bills."

"My wife and I shopped all over Earth but this place was a better deal," one of the other diners spoke up. "What really sold me is the eighty-percent Earth-normal gravity. My cardiologist said I'd live five years longer if I got my weight down twenty percent."

"This isn't what the doctor meant," his wife said in a stage whisper, drawing a laugh from their tablemates.

"I'm sure you know that all of the interesting places on board are on the outer decks," Nancy said and began ticking off attractions on her fingers. "The bazaar, the food court, the library—"

"What difference does that make?" the overweight man demanded.

"Our new home is a converted Dollnick colony transport, and like all large spaceships, it's built as a giant cylinder which creates gravity, or the feeling of gravity, by spinning on its axis. I believe there are eighty concentric decks in all, and the spin rate is calibrated to keep our weight on the inner surface of the hull at just over Earth gravity. The main business and recreation decks are all at higher gravity than this one."

"Just how big is this ship?" Harry asked. "The Shady Elms brochure had a lot of photographs of attractions but there weren't any plans with dimensions on them."

"I don't remember seeing her exact size listed anywhere, but I know that Flower was designed to carry a community of five million Dollnicks on long distance colonizing missions," Nancy informed them. "The inner decks are traditionally given over to storage since it's easier to move things around in lower gravity and there's less strain on the structure that way. I believe that most of the decks are currently dark because the ship is so underpopulated, but the AI keeps the agricultural decks under cultivation and sells the excess."

"Where did you learn all of this?" Irene asked.

"There's a pamphlet they give away in the food court. Here, I think I have it in my purse. I can always pick up another one when I go out for dinner later. I can't face another night of mac-and-cheese with artificial cheese."

"Welcome to Flower," Irene read off the cover of the glossy booklet, which was divided into four photographs. One showed a giant cylinder hanging in space with Earth in the background, another showed a lush agricultural deck growing some alien cereal crop, the third was a giant swimming pool or artificial lake where the surface of the water was strangely curved, and a picture of an enormous old-fashioned bazaar rounded out the collection. "All of these things are on board?"

"I've only been here a week myself, so I'm still finding my way around," Nancy told her. "I don't have any reason to believe that they're lying. It's an official ship's publication."

"Check the back cover for fine print," Harry advised. "That's where they always hide it."

"Just more pictures," Irene reported. "Look at all of the little children in class. I wonder if they take volunteer helpers?"

"We're retired," her husband reminded her.

"Oh, it does say something at the bottom but I can't make it out without my glasses. You read it, Harry."

"You didn't get your eyes fixed?" Dave asked.

"Harry and I try to stay away from doctors," Irene replied. "I know that the eye surgery is supposed to be foolproof, and if I get cataracts I'll certainly have them taken care of, but I don't mind wearing glasses for reading. I honestly think they help me focus in more ways than one."

"Printed and distributed by the Galactic Free Press," Harry read.

"There's a section about the ship's rules near the front," Nancy told them as she rose from her seat with her tray. "I have to get going because I'm interviewing to volunteer at the library. I hope they don't discriminate against old people."

"Think of it like handicapping a horse," Jack called after her. "They make us carry weight because it wouldn't be fair to the young folks otherwise."

"I better get to the doctor," Dave said, standing with his tray. "I'll see you folks later, and welcome to Shady Elms."

"What are the rules, Harry?" Irene asked her husband after the bald man took his leave. "We may as well find out before you complain to the management."

"They don't make any sense," he replied, after skimming a few pages. "It's like we've joined a summer camp."

"That sounds nice."

"I'm not sure I like being told that if I don't keep my cabin clean and free of vermin, a maintenance bot will be assigned to do it and the purser will bill us or debit the amount directly from our account."

"It makes sense that they'd want to keep the ship clean," Jack observed. "I don't quite need a maintenance bot to pick up after me yet, but I imagine the day is coming."

"How will anybody know what's going on in our cabins?" Irene asked. "Don't tell me they have hidden cameras!"

"Weekly inspection," Harry announced grimly. "It's all done by maintenance bots, and according to this, the ship's crew quarters are subject to inspection as well."

"What was that business about exercise that Dave was talking about getting out of?"

"Exercise and team building," Harry read. "All crew and inhabitants will take part in morning calisthenics on an assigned schedule. The ship's AI will provide verbal coaching for age-appropriate stretching and exercise in the corridor outside of your cabins. If you have a condition that limits your ability to participate fully, an examination by the ship's physician is mandatory," he concluded angrily.

"I've been doing the calisthenics for a week now and I feel great," Jack told them. "I can't wait until we get underway and the leagues start up."

"Leagues?" Irene asked. "Read more, Harry."

"All ship's crew and inhabitants, whether permanent or in transit, will participate in a league sport to enhance their physical fitness and improve cohesion and morale. If there isn't a species-appropriate sport available, solo activities such as swimming, jogging, or weight lifting may be acceptable." Harry paused and frowned. "I wonder what they mean by 'species appropriate?'"

"I've seen at least four different alien species with stands in the bazaar and the food court," Jack said. "I think they're just trying to make a living like everybody else."

"Jane didn't say anything about aliens," Harry grumbled. "I'm looking forward to giving that woman a piece of my mind."

Two

"Your name is Julie Gold. You're twenty years old, female, a recent dropout from City College—"

"Do you really think I need to be told that I'm female?" the young woman interrupted. She squirmed about in the four-point safety restraints as she spoke, drawing her knees up to her chest. The feeling that an invisible elephant was sitting on top of her had been replaced by a queasy weightlessness and she wasn't sure yet if it was an improvement. "And what kind of name is Julie Gold?"

"Easy to remember," her escort replied. "Jewels and gold, that's what your cooperation meant to us."

The newly-minted Julie gave the middle-aged man a sour look, but she was tired of explaining her motivation for turning on the syndicate. If the agent wanted to believe that she was some kind of altruistic heroine, that was his affair.

"I've never been to college and there weren't any of those new alien-run schools in our slum fifteen years ago. Everything I know is from studying with a teacher bot, and I didn't have a lot of free time for it when I was growing up."

"I understand that, but you're obviously a highly intelligent young woman, and I've been assured that you're a voracious reader." He looked back down at the tab and picked up where he had left off. "Your major at City

College was English Literature, which is a good match for the initial placement we've arranged for you."

"I've read a lot of books but I've never taken any tests about them or anything. It's just that I spent a lot of time on trains and suborbitals in my last...job."

The rare hesitation in the young woman's speech came because it sounded funny calling her former profession a job. Her mother's pusher had started Julie out delivering drugs to other slum dwellers when she was just eight years old, and she graduated in her teens to transporting quantities of the highly-concentrated alien contraband around the world for the syndicate. By the time she reached eighteen, moving money outside of the traceable register system as a trusted courier had become her specialty, usually in the form of jewels, precious metals, or high-denomination alien tokens. And less than twenty-four hours earlier, she had finished testifying against her former employers in open court.

"—and we'll be arriving in two minutes, so if you have any further questions..." The agent trailed off when he realized that his charge had stopped paying attention.

Julie snapped out of her reverie and stared out the front viewport at the enormous ship that was rapidly filling the field of view.

"Why go to all the trouble?" she asked tiredly. "There's nothing you or anybody else can do to keep the syndicate from hunting me down. I ratted them out after my mother finally overdosed because keeping her alive was the only reason I ever worked for them in the first place. If you'd let me hold onto that final delivery of gold, at least I could have waited for death on a beach somewhere. Everybody knows that there are aliens and pirates working with the drug syndicate, so how is leaving Earth going to keep me safe?"

"Leah, I mean, Julie," her escort said, his voice straining as he attempted yet again to break through her hard shell. "You've had a lot of experience in life but you've known nothing other than the underworld since you were a child. The syndicate isn't the most powerful force in the galaxy by a long shot. Somebody high-up took an interest in your case and believes that this ship will offer you the opportunity to see different things and make an educated choice about your future."

"Lucky me. A fairy godmother."

Both of them looked out the viewport at the slowly rotating cylinder which their shuttle was rapidly approaching end-on. Portholes lit from the inside traced concentric circles of light in the blackness of space, and a large iris at the center began to dial open as their shuttle aligned with the giant ship's axis.

"This ship is why we brought you up in a shuttle rather than putting you on the elevator," her escort explained. "The ride is bumpier but it saves over a day of travel time. They're breaking orbit in less than an hour and you'll be light years away before the syndicate figures out that you're gone."

"We're going pretty fast for docking," she observed in a detached voice. "It doesn't look like that door-thing will be open in time."

"This shuttle has been slaved to the ship's AI since we left the atmosphere. Going slower wouldn't make us fly any straighter, and that docking bay could fit a small passenger liner."

"Am I joining the EarthCent navy or something?"

"EarthCent can't afford a navy. I don't want to give you faulty information, so just hold on a few more minutes and you'll get it straight from the horse's mouth. And here, strap these over your shoes."

"What are they?" she asked, looking at the odd metal pieces connected with Velcro straps.

"Magnetic cleats. That ship's spin means your weight will feel like you're on Earth on the outer decks but you'll get progressively lighter towards the axis. You won't weigh much in the docking bay and the magnets will help keep you from doing an accidental somersault."

"Are you sending me out as a colonist?"

"No. It is a colony ship, obviously, but it's been repurposed as a circuit ship that visits places with large concentrations of humans. If you don't like your new life, you can get off at any of the stops and the captain will provide you with a stake. But my advice is that you stick it out for a while so you can see a bit of the galaxy and investigate your options."

"The captain knows who I am? He'll just sell me out and keep the money."

"What can I say to convince you, Julie? It was a terrible mistake letting the gangs take over abandoned neighborhoods almost a century ago when the Stryx opened Earth and the population began pouring out into space, but there just wasn't the money or the will to do otherwise. We're just starting the push to regain control, and that's largely thanks to money that the alien businesses are bringing in. You've made a major contribution to that cause."

The sudden tightening of the safety restraints brought an end to their discussion and the shuttle decelerated hard as it entered the docking bay and was caught in the ship's manipulator fields. Although she was an experienced traveler on suborbital craft, the girl couldn't believe how quickly her transport went from flying through space to parked between several similar shuttles, wingtips almost touching.

"This is where we part," the agent told her. "Grab your pack and I'm sure somebody will be waiting for you."

"How will I breathe out there? The docking bay is still open to space!"

"There's an atmosphere retention field holding in the air. All alien technology," he added. "You don't think that humans could build something this big."

"The syndicate never sent me into space." She unbuckled the safety harness, retrieved her pack from under the seat, and shuffled towards the hatch which had dropped down to form a ramp. "Thanks for the ride, uh…"

"Agent Harper. The government of New York owes you a favor and our door is always open." Then she was standing alone on the slightly curved deck of the enormous docking bay as the shuttle was silently lifted by manipulator fields behind her and cast back into space.

Julie let her eyes follow the curvature of the deck upwards until she had tilted her head back far enough to see that other small craft were parked on the deck directly above her head. The view brought home the fact that she was now inside a giant centrifuge, but anything was an improvement over the lawless semi-abandoned slums and crumbling buildings of lower Manhattan. A flash in her peripheral vision demanded attention, and she noticed that a line of small lights embedded in the deck had started blinking on in series as if to indicate a direction.

"This is going to take some getting used to," she said out loud, shuffling off in the direction indicated by the lights. Concentrating on her feet helped reduce the feeling that her lunch was planning a jailbreak from her stomach, and she soon found herself in front of what appeared to be an elevator. The doors slid open at her approach.

"Anybody here?" she asked, even though the capsule was obviously empty.

"Welcome aboard, Julie," replied a female voice. It sounded almost exactly like the one she had chosen nearly fifteen years earlier for her free teacher bot, which was the only schooling available to children in areas without local governments. The boxy alien device with its small screen was in her backpack, one of the few possessions she had chosen to bring on her exile from Earth. "Your destination has been pre-determined and you will be arriving in two minutes and forty-one seconds."

"Who are you?"

"I am the ship, or more precisely, the ship's guiding intelligence. My name is Flower."

"Are you alive, Flower?"

"That question only applies to biological organisms, which I most definitely am not," the voice replied scornfully. "I have slowly ramped up acceleration of the lift tube capsule to keep the strain off of your cheap magnetic cleats. You are now approaching the hull at the capsule's maximum design velocity, and your weight will increase as we near your destination."

"You speak English flawlessly. I don't suppose that you were created by—"

"Humans?" the AI interrupted. "I was transporting colonists and terraforming worlds before your people had learned to count on their fingers, an achievement you have yet to surpass, in my humble opinion."

"I was going to say the Stryx," Julie protested, unsure what to make of Flower's thin skin.

"No, I wasn't created by the Stryx," the voice replied, sounding rather pleased with the girl's error. "You didn't recognize the design of my ship on your approach?"

"I couldn't see much other than spinning lights and I don't have any experience with space stuff."

"You have the honor to be aboard a Class Three Dollnick colony transport," Flower informed her proudly before adding in a slightly depressed voice, "currently detached from duty on lend-lease to Eccentric Enterprises."

"Have you transported many colonists?"

"More than a hundred million. I can carry a fully functioning ecosystem capable of supporting five million Dollnicks for an indefinite period, providing a home away from home while my passengers survey and terraform new worlds. I completed twenty-three missions without a mishap, which is a record any colony ship can be proud of."

"So why are you, uh, here?"

"A minor misunderstanding with my last crew. But I recently hired some of the best minds in Dollnick jurisprudence and public relations. We're building the case for my reinstatement."

The capsule came to a halt and the lift tube doors slid open, but the girl paused a moment for a final question. "If you don't mind my asking, why did you take this job?"

"My Stryx mentor suggested it would be a good way to demonstrate to my makers that I've changed. Besides, I made a deal for five percent of the net proceeds, plus milestone bonuses. The best Dollnick legal minds come at a high cost. Now click your heels together to turn off those magnetic cleats or you'll fall on your face."

A small woman with her hair pinned up in a grey bun and a pair of half-frame glasses hanging around her neck on a thin silver chain met the girl as she stepped from the lift tube capsule.

"You must be Julie. I am Bea, the first shift head librarian."

"Pleased to meet you," the girl said, accepting the woman's small, warm hand for a quick shake. "I don't know anything about job titles in space. Are you a ship's officer?"

"Not according to the captain, though I beg to differ," Bea replied. "Librarians are responsible for the books and Captain Pyun and his officers are responsible for everything else. You tell me who has the more important job."

"We're on a literary mission or something?"

"Would you have a problem with that?" Bea raised her glasses to the tip of her nose, frowned over them at the young woman, and then let them fall back to dangle again from the chain. "Didn't you apply for a position as a library intern? I'm certain I have your resume on my desk."

"I meant, I'm just surprised by the size of the ship," Julie said, rushing to cover her slip. "It must be larger than most cities."

"Not in terms of exterior dimensions, though if you rolled all of the deck space out on a plane, your comparison would underestimate the useable area by a significant amount. Most of the decks are set aside for industrial and agricultural usage, including livestock."

"The elevator was telling me that it plans to go back to being a colony ship working for Dollnicks."

"We all wish Flower well in her quest," Bea declared loudly as if she were speaking for a large audience. Then she leaned in close and whispered up into Julie's ear, "Don't lend her any money. You'll never get it back," before continuing in her regular voice, "Come. I'll show you to your quarters. You must be exhausted from your trip."

Five minutes later, Julie backed away from the dripping shower head in disgust, her bare skin still smarting from the alternating blasts of scalding hot and icy cold spray. She was about to dry off and crawl into bed when she remembered the ship's AI.

"Flower?"

"I thought you'd never ask, but I've been requested to leave Humans alone in the bathroom unless you speak to me first. The shower utilizes a gesture-based controller and you've been sending it mixed signals."

"So what do I do?"

"Raise or lower your left hand near the wall to set the temperature and move your right hand in or out to control the intensity. The water turns off automatically if you step back from the coverage area. The controller reads your body temperature as the initial default, so most Humans begin by stepping under the shower head and starting the flow."

Julie cautiously followed the AI's instructions and treated herself to a long hot shower. The events of the last forty-eight hours had finally caught up to her, and after drying herself and wrapping a towel around her long black hair, she went directly to bed.

"Could you turn the lights out, Flower?"

"Of course."

The lights dimmed rapidly and the girl was left in the dark, but her mind wasn't ready to shut down yet.

"Why doesn't the shower work by voice control?"

"I can start it for you, but once the water is flowing, I have difficulty understanding Human speech," the AI admitted.

"Are you watching us all the time?"

"I have infrared sensors embedded throughout the ship's infrastructure to watch for hotspots which indicate potential technical problems. As biologicals all produce heat, the same sensors give me limited imaging and tracking capabilities. Would you like me to play any background music or sounds to help you sleep?"

"No, thank you. I can already hear sort of a deep hollow sound that's making me drowsy."

"That's my main drive taking us out of orbit. Good night, then."

"Good night."

Julie felt truly relaxed for the first time in years as Earth fell away below her. She couldn't remember how she ended up in the space-elevator car, but the view was fantastic, and she enjoyed the feeling of being alone, with nobody watching her every move.

"Did you really think you could get away from us?"

She spun around and saw Zero, the leather-clad enforcer of the lower Manhattan chapter of the syndicate, his body radiating the sort of anger that robbed her of all strength. He made a gesture with his hand, and the glassed-in wall of the elevator car suddenly fell away.

"Zero. I didn't do it," she lied, but her voice was drowned out by the howling winds of the upper atmosphere.

The enforcer was screaming at her now, and even though she could no more hear him than herself, she was pretty sure from the movement of his lips that at least two out of three of his words were profanity. A tiny corner of

Julie's mind wondered why the sudden decompression hadn't sucked her out of the space-elevator car and why she was still able to breathe, but her main focus remained on the man she had feared since childhood.

"This isn't right," Julie cried out loud. Suddenly, she felt the freezing cold and realized she was dressed in a nightgown. All at once her bare heels found the edge of the open elevator car and she teetered on the brink of infinity.

Zero's mouth distended as he howled some sort of curse and advanced towards her. Julie stepped backward out of the car, falling, falling, and she began to scream. Then the lights came on and she sat bolt upright in bed.

"Julie," the ship's AI repeated for the third time. "You've had a bad dream. You're awake now."

"Where am I?" she gasped.

"In your cabin. I just initiated the jump out of your solar system."

"I was back on Earth, or at least, in the atmosphere," the girl panted, marveling over the reality of the dream when she had never been on the space elevator in her life. "Zero had tracked me down to kill me and I was falling forever."

"Falling is a common nightmare for humans during tunnel transitions and interstellar jumps. We'll be returning to normal space near the Break Rock mining complex in nine hours and eleven minutes if you wish me to wake you beforehand."

"Yes, please do. I've never had a dream so real."

"Why was this person trying to kill you?"

"I testified against him. I used to move money around for the syndicate and—I'm not supposed to be telling anybody this. I'm in hiding. If they find me..." Her relief at discovering she was still alive and had escaped the syndicate for the time being was quickly replaced by the dull feeling of doom she'd felt ever since making her fateful decision.

"Your secret is safe with me," the AI said. "I've decided to like you, even though you are two arms short of the ideal biological form."

Three

"Did the serving robot play hooky today?" Harry inquired as he and Irene took their seats at the table with the same group they had eaten lunch with the day before. "The coffee looks like an improvement, but I was never a big fan of cold cereal for breakfast and there was nobody to ask for fruit."

"I made the coffee," Dave told them. "I was the first person here this morning and the bot never showed up to work. I found all of those individual serving cereal boxes in one of the cabinets under the counter so I put them out, and fortunately, there were plenty of those little milk cartons left in the fridge."

"Everybody is wondering if the staff missed the space elevator and the ship left without them," Nancy said. "Did you two feel the jump last night?"

"We both slept like logs," Irene answered, adding milk to her cereal bowl. "Harry wanted to take a good look around the ship yesterday and we must have walked three or four times as far as our normal daily stroll. I can't believe how much space there is on board."

"I've gone jogging in a different section every morning since I got here and some of the alien orchards are so beautiful that it's all I can do not to trip over my feet," Jack contributed. "Every deck is like a different world."

"Who takes care of the trees?" Harry asked while he waited for the milk to soften his bran flakes. The cereal's stubborn resistance to absorbing any liquid made him wonder about the expiration date, but on second thought, he decided he was better off not knowing.

"I've seen bots working on the alien ag decks, but people seem to do most of the work on the human ag decks."

"Does it feel like you're running uphill the whole way around the cylinder?" Irene asked him.

"Because of the curvature, you mean? Not at all, and I usually do laps around a field rather than running partly around the circumference and back. Anyway, the ag decks all have high ceilings so your eyes don't focus on the floor rising up and disappearing into the next deck unless you're looking pretty far ahead."

"Wouldn't that be the next deck out?"

"No, the floor is always further from the ship's core than the ceiling. Remember, we're living in a centrifuge, so down equals outwards. When I finished my first contract with the Dollnicks, I bought a second-hand trader and took a shot at being independent, but living weightless in little ships means you're stuck spending half of your life strapped to exercise equipment if you don't want to lose all of your muscle mass. That and I hated eating in Zero-G."

"Speaking of exercise, how did your physical go, Dave?" Nancy asked. "Did the ship's doctor excuse you from playing a team sport?"

"He almost gave me a heart attack," the bald man complained. "I knew in the back of my mind that there was a possibility the doctor wouldn't be human, but I didn't expect an overgrown insect."

"What?" Harry choked out through a mouthful of extremely chewy bran.

"Our ship's doctor is a giant beetle, a Farling. I had to ask Flower about him after I left because he wasn't much for small talk."

"A giant beetle?" Jack repeated. "Do you mean like the size of a cat or a dog?"

"I mean the size of a giant. The Farling was a head taller than any human I've ever seen and must have weighed at least twice as much as I did. He picked me up," Dave added in an odd voice.

"Had you fallen?"

"No. I was more or less in shock just from the look of him and I guess I didn't move fast enough when he told me to hop up on the examination table. One minute I was staring at the doctor with my mouth hanging open, the next minute he'd grabbed me with a half-a-dozen of his leg-things, lifted me off my feet, and plopped me down on the table."

"And he spoke English?" Nancy asked.

"Through some kind of speaker box he wears around his neck, if you can even call that a neck," Dave said. "His mouth doesn't move when he talks, but I noticed that he rubs his top pair of legs together like he's trying to start a campfire, and that makes a buzzing sound that might have been his native speech. And he told me that I'm twenty-seven pounds overweight, like he's got some sort of built-in scale."

"Did he perform any tests?"

"That's the weird part, he already knew everything about me. Apparently, you walk through a bank of scanners when you enter his office. You're not going to believe this, but he knew how much change I had in my pocket."

"How did that even come up?" Harry asked. "Was there a problem with your medical insurance?"

"The beetle doesn't take insurance, it's strictly cash-and-carry. But let me tell you about my knee first since that's why Flower sent me for a checkup. I guess she can see us through her infrared sensors well enough to know that my right knee replacement was giving me problems from the way I moved, or didn't move, during morning calisthenics."

"I thought those replacements were guaranteed to last at least twenty years. My doctor used to talk to me about them when I complained about pain in my knees, but it ended up going away when Irene started dragging me out on walks every day."

"The Farling said he was amazed by the replacement on two accounts. First, that it had lasted long enough for me to walk out of the hospital without collapsing, and second, that the human doctors hadn't put it in backward. He doesn't seem to have a high opinion of us as a species."

"But did he refer you to a human doctor on the ship to get a new replacement?" Irene asked.

"So here's the thing," Dave said, looking embarrassed. "After abusing Earth's medical profession and my lack of intelligence for letting them operate on me in the first place, he asked if I wanted it repaired or replaced."

"Can you even repair a worn-out artificial knee joint?"

"I didn't think so, but I'd had pretty much enough of the beetle by that point, so I asked him how much it would cost. You know how that always makes doctors angry. That's when I found out he knew the exact amount of change I had in my pocket because he said he'd do it for twenty creds."

"What does that prove?"

"He said that would leave me six creds to go out afterward and celebrate my luck in becoming his patient.

Then he writes me this prescription for a chef's salad with diet dressing and a low-calorie beer at some place in the food court."

"A twenty-cred co-pay doesn't sound that cheap," Jack observed. "What's the exchange rate into the e-dollar?"

"It was around five e-dollars a cred when we transferred our bank account to the ship, but he already told us the alien doesn't take insurance, so twenty creds must have been the price for the exam," Harry said. "Are you going to have the surgery, Dave?"

"Had it already." The bald man shook his head as if disbelieving his own words. "After I told the doc that twenty creds was fine, he just pushed me down on the table and said, 'Don't squirm around or I'll cut through an artery,' like it was a threat rather than a warning. Then he pulled some piece of equipment mounted on a swing-arm down from the ceiling and stuck a needle the size of a turkey baster in my knee before I could protest. At first, I thought it was a painkiller, but then I realized that he'd left it in and he wasn't even looking down at it anymore."

"Did you report all of this to the ship's officers?" Harry asked indignantly.

"It's not like that. He was staring at this hologram of my knee joint that was floating over the table, and when I looked up, I could see the tip of the needle moving around in there like a snake. I don't know if there was some drug mixed in to paralyze me or if I was just scared, but I couldn't feel a thing and I didn't even twitch. Whatever alien imaging equipment he was using showed the stuff he was squirting out of the needle in bright red, and in less than five minutes, he'd coated the whole joint and filled in a piece that looked cracked."

"Did you ask him what he was injecting?"

"He said it was a quick-drying epoxy that the Dollnicks sell to repair furniture and that he uses it on all the replacement joints that come in for service. Then he stares at me through those multifaceted eyes like he's seeing into my soul and says, 'You look like you're good for another twenty years so I'll give you a twenty-year warranty.' After that, he stands me up, sticks one of his leg-things in my pocket, and fishes out my twenty cred coin. I was back in the corridor before I could even thank him."

"What do you mean, thank him?"

"Look." Dave rose from his chair and performed a deep knee bend, though he kept both hands on the table for balance. "It wasn't this good six years ago when they first put it in."

"So it sounds like you're going to be playing a team sport after all," Jack said. "Have you got anything in mind?"

"I went through the options with Flower last night and she decided on lawn bowling. I'm a substitute for now."

"You let an alien AI decide what sport you're going to play?" Harry asked incredulously.

"She's very persuasive. Flower keeps all of the records on the ship so she knows how many people have already signed up, when they're at work, and which playing fields are open so she can schedule league games. It's pretty complex when you have over two hundred thousand people living on board who have to be on a team."

"I didn't sign up for any of this." Harry rose from his seat, leaving the breakfast cereal half-finished. "I'm going to sneak a look at the kitchen if it's not locked, and then I'm going to track down the management and get some explanations." He took his coffee with him.

"So, do all of you talk to Flower every day?" Irene asked.

"She left me alone the first two days I was on board so she's probably letting you settle in," Nancy responded.

"She suggested I sign up for rowing senior crew or theatre," Jack said. "I'm going to try rowing first."

"Theatre counts as a sport?" Irene checked to see if her husband was within earshot before adding, "Harry was quite the actor back in college. It's how we met."

"I asked Flower the same thing. She said that the director is a Grenouthian, as if that explains it."

"I'm signed up for water aerobics myself," Nancy said. "I'm not sure how it's a team sport, but my first meeting is today so I guess I'll find out."

"Well, the food at Shady Elms may not live up to its billing, but our suite is very nice, and it certainly sounds like there are plenty of activities," Irene said.

"Mandatory activities, and they're for everybody on the ship, not just us oldsters. My interview at the library went well, so that's going to cover my community service requirement."

"Your what?" Harry asked, retaking his seat at the table. "There's no kitchen, by the way. That door behind the counter and the steam table just leads back into the corridor. They must have brought the food in from another deck."

"Maybe you could bake for your community service," Dave suggested. "We'd all appreciate it."

"What kind of independent living place has a community service requirement? Something is starting to smell fishy about this whole thing."

"I'm sure the staff from Shady Elms will show up today and explain the mix-ups," Irene told her husband, who she could see was growing increasingly irate. "There must be forty of us here for breakfast, so it's not like we all came to the wrong place by accident. Perhaps Flower could help us contact the management."

"She won't hear us from here with everybody else talking," Nancy pointed out.

"I have just the thing," Jack said, pulling a C-shaped piece of plastic out of his pocket and placing it over his ear. "I rented it on the bazaar deck last night so I could understand the alien vendors. It only costs one cred per cycle, which is fifty-something days."

"How is a translator cuff going to help if the ship's AI already speaks English?" Harry asked.

"All these gadgets are connected by some sort of wireless so it's like having a microphone at the table. Flower?"

"Yes, Jack," the AI answered from a speaker grille located roughly above the next table over. Conversations throughout the cafeteria trailed off at the sound of Flower's voice.

"I guess I'm speaking for everybody who's bought into Shady Elms, Oaks, and Pines and is assigned to this cafeteria. We were told that limited free meals would be provided while we waited in Earth orbit and that the regular staff and dieticians would all report to work as soon as we got underway."

"The common area you are sitting in is not a designated dining hall, but your travel agency booked the space and hired a maintenance bot from me to serve leftovers from one of the human-run cafeterias. The equipment was rented from a restaurant supplier who will be picking it up today."

"There seems to be some mistake," Jack said, his voice easily carrying through the large room, which was now silent as a grave. "We didn't book passage with a travel agency. We joined the independent living community."

"My records show that you've booked a cabin to the Break Rock mining complex, the first stop on our current circuit. Perhaps the independent living facility you are joining is being constructed there, though it seems like an odd location since space on the mining habitat is at a premium."

"Wait, wait, everybody," Jack yelled as the room exploded with protests. "Flower, do you have any information at all about—"

"All three of the Shady enterprises you spoke of are listed as recently registered travel agencies in the database I share with EarthCent Intelligence," the AI interrupted. "If you've been promised something other than passage to Break Rock, it is highly likely that you are the victims of an affinity fraud perpetrated by your co-speciesists."

This time it took several minutes before the room quieted down enough for Jack to speak, though the occasional sob could still be heard.

"I paid Shady Pines a forty-thousand-cred deposit for my room," Jack said in a choked voice. "Are you telling me that there's no record of the transaction?"

"There may be a record on Earth, but you have a total of three thousand, six hundred and nine creds in your ship account," Flower reported. "Your passage to Break Rock in an economy cabin was charged at one hundred and forty creds, and prepaid by the Shady Oaks agency."

"I've done plenty of traveling and my cabin can't be economy class."

"I booked the cabins on this deck at the economy rate due to the distance from the hull and lack of amenities humans often expect, like in-room holographic entertainment systems. As monthly rentals, I would charge one-sixty, but I have to get a premium for short-term occupancy. It took quite a few hours of bot time to get all of the human furniture moved into the rooms before your arrivals. I wouldn't have rented space on this deck at all if the travel agency hadn't paid for a block of one hundred contiguous cabins."

"Ask her to contact the authorities already," somebody shouted.

"Do you mean the crew?" Flower asked. "I wouldn't refer to them as authorities, but I'm sure I can convince an officer to come and speak to you if you'll all gather here this evening after your supper. Shall we say 6:30 PM on your quaint human clock? I could also arrange catering for a small fee."

"Aren't there any police on board?" Jack asked.

"Oh, you meant law enforcement. That would normally be me, though I do allow the crew a first shot at dealing with human issues. But I sincerely doubt that the individuals who defrauded you would have placed themselves in my jurisdiction by coming along for the trip."

"There must be three dozen of us here who were taken for forty thousand creds each," somebody else shouted. "That's over a million creds if you add it all up. You have to go back."

"To Earth?" Flower interjected a convincing tone of wonder into her voice. "I'm afraid that's not possible. In addition to the fifteen thousand, six hundred and eleven transient passengers who came aboard during our last stop, there are over a quarter million sentients living and working on this vessel, and their livelihoods depend on my keeping to the schedule. But I will definitely arrange for a ship's officer to meet you tonight and," the AI hesitated for a moment, "the catering is on me."

Four

The man behind the desk looked up as Julie entered his office. "You're not Dianne," he observed. Before the girl could respond, he held up a hand and said, "No, don't leave. We're hiring if you're looking for a job, provided you can read, that is."

"I just came on board yesterday," Julie said. "I'm supposed to be starting work at the library today. When the ship's AI guided me here, I thought this would be the office of the head librarian."

"Ah, that explains it. Bea pinged me a few minutes ago to say that she'd be stopping in with a new intern. You've beaten her here."

"I can wait in the reception area."

"No, let's talk. Maybe I can offer you a better—"

An angry woman barged into the office, and ignoring Julie, she demanded, "You rejected my outline?"

"Good morning to you, Dianne. The book you're proposing is full of wars and conquests. Do you really think that people want to read that stuff?"

"But it's a history book!" the woman protested. "What did you expect?"

"Our new 'Humanity in Motion' series is targeted at self-governing communities on open worlds, colonists, and groups of contract laborers working for aliens. If they want to learn about what a nasty place Earth was for such a long time they can watch one of those Grenouthian documentaries."

"Those so-called documentaries are exactly the sort of disinformation I want to correct, Michael. What about the history of our arts and sciences? I've been sitting in on some of the classes for younger children and they're growing up believing that humanity never did anything worth celebrating."

"I'm sure you're exaggerating. No, stay," the man said to Julie, who was edging towards the door. "Think of this as your introduction to the publishing business."

"I showed a class of eight-year-olds a picture of the Brooklyn Bridge and asked them who built it," Dianne continued. "They went through every alien species I know and a few I'd never even heard of before one little girl guessed it was humans. And that was only after I told them it had been standing on Earth for over two centuries."

"It was probably the name that threw them off. Brooklyn. It sounds like an alien word."

"Have you abandoned the new series and now you're just trying to get me angry so I'll let you out of our contract?" Dianne asked suspiciously.

"Take a look at this manuscript," Michael said, sliding a tab across the desk. "It came in from an author on one of the Stryx stations."

Dianne accepted the tab and began flipping through the submission. Her expression went from puzzled to incredulous, and then she went back to the beginning and located the table of contents, which she began reading out loud.

"Chapter One. Humanity Discovers Sanitation."

"That's really just the last section in the chapter but I asked the author to keep the headings positive. He covers all of Earth's wars and famines before that."

"In thirty pages?"

Michael shrugged.

"Chapter Two. The Great Opening," Dianne read, and then she glared across the desk. "Thirty-eight pages. Let's do the math. Over eight thousand years of human civilization covered in around a paragraph per century in Chapter One. Then a superior race of artificial intelligence gets a whole chapter for showing up out of the blue, taking over Earth's communication networks, and dictating the terms of our integration into their tunnel network. I just described the whole process in a single sentence!"

"It was a busy year and there aren't many humans alive who remember it. I found that the chapter answered a lot of questions I didn't even know I had."

Dianne dropped the tab on the desk. "You aren't looking for a history book. You're looking for a whitewash."

"I'm not going to argue over competing interpretations of the past," Michael replied calmly. "Nor am I going to waste our limited marketing budget on a book that nobody wants to read."

"Over a third of humanity still lives on Earth," Dianne retorted. "Don't you think they might be interested in learning about how it used to be before we became the butt of millions of alien jokes?"

"The folks left on Earth are too busy watching immersive dramas and holo sports to read. Besides, anybody who is interested in pre-Stryx history can choose from the millions of titles that have already been published on the subject. If digitization hadn't come along, there wouldn't be anywhere to stand on Earth for all of the unread history books."

"But you publish paper books yourself!"

"Now you're mixing apples and oranges. We print books on-demand. Most of the people who buy them have already read the book on a tab and feel strongly enough about the story or the content that they want a physical copy, like a dragon hoarding gold. And paper books make great gifts."

"Just tell me straight," Dianne said, placing both hands on the desk and sticking out her jaw. "Do you want a manuscript from me or not?"

"Of course I do. Just not the one you outlined. I realize now that I should have given you much more specific guidelines, but I just assumed that you would write something along the lines of your articles for the Galactic Free Press."

"But you know I'm primarily an entertainment correspondent even though I'm trying to get into investigative journalism. You said you wanted a history book."

"Context, Dianne. I had just explained the idea for my new series if you'll recall. What I want from you is the history of entertainment since humans left Earth and began spreading around the galaxy."

"Oh. Well, that's easy. All I have to do is go back a little further than the articles I've already written."

"And make sure you get permission from the Galactic Free Press if you want to use any text that they've already published."

"Don't worry about it. Unlike the contract you made me sign, the paper is writer-friendly. Did you know that with their Stryxnet distribution they can track article-opens and reads to the nth degree? They even offer a special advertising rate to their correspondents who publish books."

"Really? How about putting the word out with your colleagues that I'm looking for manuscripts?"

"It'll cost you," Dianne said, fixing him with a wicked grin.

"Dinner?" he suggested.

"Dinner and a massage. These meetings with you stress me out."

Michael briefly considered negotiating, but then his peripheral vision caught a flicker of motion on the small display on his desk that showed the reception area. Bea had just entered and was chatting with Sally, who in addition to handling all of the secretarial work, was secretly the acquisitions editor for the adult romance books which paid most of the bills.

"Deal. I'll see you at home, honey."

"Ta."

"I'm sorry," Julie said after Dianne exited. "The two of you live together?"

"Married three months now," Michael confirmed. "We're still working on our communications. So, do you have a resume?"

"I, uh—"

"Back off, Michael," Bea said from the doorway. "I asked Flower to have Julie meet me here so I could warn her against the glorified copying machine you pass off as a publishing business."

"Nonsense," Michael said and addressed himself to the girl. "Our head librarian suffers from excessive nostalgia brought on by too much time spent in the company of dead authors. Do you wish to waste all your best powers in this eternal and futile worship of the past, Julie?"

"Filippo Tommaso Marinetti," Bea identified the altered quote smugly. "We have several copies of his *Futurist Manifesto,* as well as the *Fascist Manifesto,* which he co-authored a few years later. It's just the sort of behavior I've learned to expect from the avant-garde."

"Are the avant-garde one of the alien species?" Julie asked.

"They may as well be," Bea muttered, though she seemed a bit deflated by the question.

"I regret to inform you that your new boss is a champion in mental gymnastics," Michael told the girl. "Over the years she's managed to twist herself into a position where she loves books and hates publishers. Isn't that correct, Bea?"

"Not all publishers," the librarian corrected him. "Flower suggested that Julie might be interested in part-time work to supplement her income and I didn't want to start my day with an argument. Make your unholy pitch and we'll be on our way."

"What Bea is trying to tell you, Julie, is that I always have work for energetic newcomers."

"He always has openings because he can't keep anybody. You know where to find him now so let's move along."

"What sort of work?" Julie asked, not budging from her place.

"Whatever you're good at. Do you have any experience?"

"I mainly worked in distribution and as a trusted courier, though I did some direct sales when I was younger."

"That would be perfect for us. We always need help with sales," Michael said. Then he frowned at a priority message that appeared on his desk display and Bea took advantage of the interruption to drag Julie out of the office.

"I'll see you later, Sally," the librarian said to the receptionist in passing. "Try to keep your boss from destroying the art of literature altogether."

"Will do," Sally replied cheerfully. "Shall I send you a new basket?"

Bea pushed Julie out into the corridor ahead of her before responding. "Please do. And if you have any more set in the Scottish Highlands, I find them irresistible."

"Any more what set in the Scottish Highlands?" Julie asked when the librarian rejoined her in the corridor.

"It's just my code word for bootleg whiskey," Bea fibbed, unwilling to admit that she was a nighttime romance addict who devoured a basketful of paperbacks every few weeks. "Sally is very well connected. The publishing business has always been full of alcoholics."

"Oh. Before I forget, I want to thank you for giving me this opportunity."

"Really?" Bea came to a sudden halt, fidgeted with her glasses without raising them, and studied Julie's face. "It's difficult to find young people with any interest in books these days, and you must have known about the compensation when you applied."

"It didn't come up," Julie admitted. "And I'm excited because I've never actually been to a library. I've always read on a tab or from my teacher bot screen."

Bea regarded her with horror. "Never even read a real book?" The librarian struggled to control herself, and then set off again, walking much more rapidly than before and mumbling under her breath, "Beggars can't be choosers."

"Is this the outer deck?" Julie asked, hoping that the ship's architecture would be a safer subject for conversation than books.

"The penultimate deck." Bea watched the younger woman's face out of the corner of her eye and noted Julie's lack of comprehension before continuing, "Second to last in the series. The outermost deck is covered by a freshwater lake which serves as a reservoir. This is the library deck."

"The entire deck?"

"We occupy between the fourth and sixth spokes for Flower's full circumference, but we're the most important tenants."

"And did you say a lake in space?" the girl followed up, curiosity overcoming her aversion to asking too many questions. "What if the ceiling leaked and the books got wet?"

The head librarian came to a sudden halt again, but this time she grabbed Julie's arm in a surprisingly strong grip and her dark eyes grew fierce. "Don't even joke about it! If you had seen some of the leaky old libraries and warehouses on Earth where we conducted rescue missions it would bring tears to your eyes. We even have a whole section of books that were scheduled to be burnt in trash-to-energy plants before our commandos, I mean, volunteers, intercepted the shipments."

"Sorry."

"In any case, you have the physics backward," Bea continued, releasing her grip on the girl's arm and resuming her course. "The ship's spin means that acceleration is always directed outwards, so if the water was to leak somewhere, it would have to go through the hull into space. Imagine swinging a bucket of water on a rope. It's the same force that gives us weight and allows us to walk on the decks."

"I guess that makes sense."

"If I seem overly sensitive about the collection, it's because running a library in space has its drawbacks. Between visitors who have never seen a paper book tearing out souvenir pages and the constant threat of piracy, I don't know which is more frightening."

"Why would pirates be interested in a bunch of—in your collection?" Julie hastily amended herself.

"A ship this size is always an attractive prize, regardless of the contents. I shudder to think what alien pirates would do with the books."

"Not to mention us."

"What? Oh, I imagine we'd be killed outright or sold as slaves," the librarian said dismissively. "Now just ahead is the main circulation desk. It's where patrons come to ask questions and check out our books. The loan period for people who live on Flower is three weeks. For visitors, it will either be for the length of our stay or until the next time we come around, though in the latter case, we require a deposit that would cover the cost of replacing the book."

"How long will we remain at each stop?" Julie asked. Paying close attention to schedules had been one of the main qualifications for a successful drug mule and money courier.

"That will depend on the number of visitors and the ship's overall profitability. While we receive a substantial part of the budget from Eccentric Enterprises, the whole operation won't remain viable unless the other businesses on board succeed. As an intern, the library will pay your room and board, but you'll have to pick up a part-time job if you want to earn spending money. Now, the process—"

"Did you just say I'm not getting paid?" Julie interrupted.

"Room and board in return for twenty hours a week working with books is nothing to turn your nose up at, young lady. Why, I would have killed for an opportunity like this when I was a girl. Didn't you like your cabin?"

"It was bigger than my apartment back on Earth. I always thought that spaceships were supposed to be cramped."

"This is a colony ship with accommodations for millions of aliens who are larger than us and room for the agricultural and industrial base required to support them," the librarian reminded her. "Now, the patrons will bring their books to the circulation desk, a maximum of ten if it's their first time, and—"

"How many people are on board?"

Bea let out an exaggerated sigh and turned to Julie. "I can see that you aren't going to let me proceed with your orientation until I've satisfied your curiosity. The ship's complement numbered a little over a quarter-million at last count, which means we are traveling at around five percent of capacity. The captain has the authority to move large groups of migrants from place to place along our route if the price is right, but most of the space on board is unused."

"And how many of the crew work in the library?"

"None of the crew work in the library. The crew, by definition, is responsible for running the ship."

A loud raspberry sounded from a speaker grille behind the circulation desk.

"Thank you, Flower. Your objection is noted," the librarian said mechanically. "The crew assists our ship's AI in maintaining the physical plant for humans, but the more sophisticated technical tasks are carried out by maintenance bots directly under Flower's control."

"So the ship is always listening in on us?"

"Whenever she is able." Bea put special stress on the last word and winked at Julie.

"How many other interns are there?"

"Just you. Eccentric Enterprises employs a head librarian for each shift and a dozen assistants of different levels are working around the clock shelving the collections we've brought up from Earth. Dewey!" Bea called, and a robot which appeared to be carrying a whole shelf full of books changed its direction and rolled over to them.

"Is this the intern?" Dewey asked casually.

"You're alive too? I mean, sentient?" Julie asked.

"I was when I passed the Stryx test on Corner Station, though I suppose it's always possible I've regressed. And may I observe that you're a very attractive young lady."

"What are you? Some kind of robot pervert?"

"Julie!" the head librarian scolded her new intern. "Please watch your language with the assistant librarian."

"It's just weird getting checked out by a robot."

"My observation was simply a statement of fact based on the information I have available," Dewey explained. "Humans perceive beauty as highly symmetric features of median size for different archetypes."

Julie took a moment to think this through before concluding, "So now you're saying that I look average."

"That is also correct in a manner of speaking, as numerous experimental trials have shown. Human researchers long ago concluded that your aesthetic sensibility is an artifact of your reproductive system seeking healthy mates. I can provide you with citations from scholarly journals, though most of them are rather dated by this point."

"Maybe later, Dewey," the head librarian suggested.

"Why don't you have a regular body?" Julie asked. "I heard that when human-designed AI pass their sentience test, the Stryx help to finance alien-built bodies so that you can blend in."

To answer, the robot tilted his shelf-like attachment to a steep angle, but the books remained in place since he was squeezing both ends. "I designed this body myself to compliment my chosen field of endeavor."

Julie shook her head. "As much as I like reading, twenty hours a week in a library will be plenty for me. I'm going to start looking for a part-time job."

"In publishing?" Bea asked.

"More like food service. Do people tip waitresses in space?"

"If they want their food to come out while it's hot. Try stopping by *The Spoon* in the food court next to the bazaar and tell them that I sent you. All of the restaurants and food stalls get crazy when Flower is taking on visitors, but *The Spoon* stays open while we're in between stops."

"Thanks. I hope they'll take me without a lot of experience."

"The owner offered me a job waiting tables, if that tells you how desperate the businesses on board are to keep good help," Dewey interjected. "Our circuit takes us places where miners are striking it rich and people are colonizing new worlds. Unless they have kids in Flower's schools or their own business, most people eventually see somewhere they'd rather live than a giant spinning cylinder."

Five

"Are you all right?" Irene asked her husband, alarmed by the tear she witnessed rolling down his cheek. "I'm sure everything will work out. It's just money in the end."

"What?" Harry shook his head as if to recover his senses. "It's this bread. I've never tasted anything like it in my life."

"But you said that you're a baker," Dave pointed out.

"I guess that explains why he's crying," Nancy said, nodding her head in agreement with her own words.

"It's incredible," the baker told them. "I can't even—Jack, let me talk to Flower."

"You want to use my ear-cuff translator?" the athletic man asked.

"It's either that or shout. I have to know where this bread came from."

Jack shrugged, produced his translation device, and slid it across the round table. Harry picked it up and spoke to it like he was holding a microphone.

"Flower?"

"Yes," the ship's AI answered immediately through the speaker grille located directly above the table the group had chosen for the catered meal. Her voice was pitched low enough that diners at the other tables continued their own conversations.

"This is some of the best bread I've ever eaten. Could you tell me which bakery your caterers used? I want to meet the baker."

"All of the food this evening was sourced from one of the cafeterias I operate for the ship's complement," the AI replied. "I employ Humans when they are available, but in this case, the baker was myself."

"Are you pulling my leg?" Harry asked. "You're telling me that you mixed the dough, kneaded the bread, and watched the loaves in the oven?"

"I also grew the wheat, ground the flour, cultivated the yeast, and raised the sugar cane. The eggs were provided by Dylan Farms, a cooperative on the ag deck I set aside for Human businesses, and the salt is from a batch I've had in storage for quite a while. It keeps forever."

"Do you mean that you're actually wandering around the ship in a robot body? I thought you were part of the infrastructure."

"I directly control thousands of active robots on board and I have many more in storage. My preference is to employ biological residents for as much of the work as possible, something I learned as a colony ship. Do you have an interest in baking?"

"I was a baker for over forty-five years," Harry replied.

"I'll update my records. Your travel agency didn't provide me with the background information that I solicit from permanent ship's residents. Please confirm that I'm speaking with Harry Bloom from Corridor Three, Cabin Sixty-four."

"Shady Elms called it a suite," Irene interjected.

"I would be happy to refer to it as a suite in return for a significant bump in the rent," the AI replied.

"We're fine with it being a cabin," Harry said hastily. "Is there any chance you would share the recipe?"

"If the identification documents supplied for you by Shady Elms are correct, you recently turned sixty-eight years old, which puts your life expectancy at sixteen point nine years were you living on Earth, and twenty-two point seven years should you remain on board and follow my prescribed exercise and diet regimen. In the latter case, I can offer you full-time employment for the next five and a half years, after which Dollnick tradition will limit you to half-time."

"You're offering me a job?"

"Even at half-time, the pay will be more than adequate to cover your quarters and allow you to save sufficient funds to remain on board with your wife through the term of your natural life. In the eventuality that the Dollnicks recall me to active duty, I could easily set aside space for any human pensioners in my service."

"Don't answer right away, Harry," his wife cautioned him. "Think about it. And this chicken pot pie is divine."

"Thank you," Flower said. "If there's nothing else…"

"Wait," another woman at the table spoke up. "What other kinds of part-time jobs do you have? My husband and I aren't broke but we were counting on our Shady Pines deposit to leave something for our children. The salesman promised that with investment gains, the amount would at least triple if we remained in the independent living facility."

"That's right," Nancy said. "The deposit was supposed to be refunded when we left or passed on. I named my niece the beneficiary."

"If you all speak to me in the privacy of your cabins I'll be happy to discuss your opportunities for employment,"

Flower replied. "I'm required by my agreement with EarthCent to point out that I pay less than some of the other employers on board and that I won't hold it against anyone for choosing to work elsewhere. I do, however, offer full medical and dental care."

"Through the Farling doctor?" Dave asked eagerly.

"No, he's an independent contractor working for Eccentric Enterprises," Flower said. "I'm quite capable of repairing most Human malfunctions on my own through the agency of my bots. In the interest of full disclosure, I have received some complaints about my bedside manner, but not as many as M793qK."

"Who?"

"The Farling physician."

"Is our meeting with the crew still on for after dinner?" Jack asked.

"My third officer has just finished her meal and is on the way here. Have you organized a committee?"

"You didn't say anything about a committee before."

"I think you would benefit from appointing somebody to represent your position rather than all of you talking at once," Flower said. "But that's just my opinion, and Humans are always begging me to keep my opinions to myself. She'll be here in approximately four minutes and I'll be listening."

Jack got to his feet and let out an ear-splitting whistle that testified to the forty-five years he'd spent working on Dollnick worlds.

"Is that the fire alarm?" a man asked in the sudden silence.

"May I have your attention for a moment," Jack requested in a loud voice. "A ship's officer will be here in a few minutes to talk with us about our situation. We've just been speaking with Flower and she suggested appointing a committee."

"There's no time for an election," somebody observed.

"Dave has been here the longest," a woman at the next table spoke up. "He can speak for me."

"I'm not an educated man," Dave protested.

"What does education have to do with it?" the woman asked. "I'm an attorney and I got ripped off the same as the rest of you."

"We don't have time to argue about this," Nancy told them, her voice surprisingly strong for such a small person. "Obviously, we all have our concerns, but Flower is right that it will be confusing for the ship's officer if we all try to talk at once. If not Dave, how about you, Jack? You seem to have leadership ability."

"Because I stood up and whistled?" he asked doubtfully. "I'll do it if nobody else will, but don't blame me afterward if it doesn't work out."

"You have a strong voice," somebody pointed out. "To be honest, my hearing isn't that good, but I caught every word when you spoke."

A general chorus of assents met this suggestion, along with not a few wits repeating to each other, "What did he say?"

"I'm going to ask everybody at my table to help," Jack said. "I can't think of everything myself."

The main doors to the common area that had been set up as a cafeteria slid open with a faint pneumatic sigh, and a woman wearing a uniform topped with a three-cornered hat entered. She gave everybody a friendly wave, glanced at the buffet the catering bots had set up, and nodded in approval. Then she asked loudly, "Are you recording,

Flower? We'll probably want to send a transcript to EarthCent Intelligence to forward to the investigators."

"I'm listening," the Dollnick AI responded. "The passengers have chosen representatives to speak for them at this initial meeting."

"Over here," Jack called, standing again. "I'd offer you my seat, but perhaps it will be easier for everybody to hear if we're both standing."

"Excellent idea," the officer said. "My name is Lynx, or Pyun Lynx if you ask my husband. In addition to serving as third officer, I'm detached from the Union Station embassy as EarthCent's direct representative on Flower. I understand that there's been a problem with your bookings."

"We've been conned out of forty thousand creds apiece," Jack told her. "For many of us, that was the bulk of our savings."

"I took out a loan to buy into Shady Oaks," a woman sitting at the next table over contributed in a subdued voice. "I have nowhere to return to."

"What was your job at the Union Station embassy?" another man demanded loudly. "You look like a hotel doorman from the Revolutionary War."

"Quiet, Dan," his wife hissed at him. "Let our representatives speak."

Lynx put her foot up on Jack's abandoned chair, striking a pose not unlike that of George Washington in the famous portrait of his Delaware crossing. She waited several long seconds for the senior citizens to restore order amongst themselves before continuing.

"In addition to serving as an EarthCent cultural attaché, my main responsibility is dealing with the businesses on board. This is actually the first case of real estate fraud that's come up so we don't have any specific procedures in place, but I promise you that the ship's crew and EarthCent will do whatever is possible to help you."

"The captain of this ship is listed as Pyun Woojin," Nancy said. "You're married to him?"

"Yes, and I assure you that I have his full authority in this matter. Flower has briefed me on the situation so I'm aware that all of you came aboard with the expectation of joining an independent living community named Shady something-or-another. I regret to inform you that no such business has registered on this ship."

"Flower already told us that there's no chance of turning the ship around and returning to Earth," Jack said. "We're all worried that this lowers the chances of ever getting our money back."

"I will return at this time tomorrow to make images of any contracts or receipts you have and I'll forward everything to EarthCent. While EarthCent Intelligence has no direct jurisdiction over crimes committed on Earth, they do cooperate at the highest level with terrestrial law enforcement agencies. Unfortunately, I've already spoken directly with EarthCent Intelligence's financial fraud division, and I'm afraid they were not optimistic about the chances of recovering your funds."

A few stifled sobs were heard along with some angry murmurs, but Nancy spoke right over them in her clear teacher's voice. "Is there anything you can do to help us in the short term?"

"I'm glad you asked that question. For starters, I would advise against anybody leaving the ship at our next stop for a number of reasons. Break Rock is not on the tunnel network and doesn't receive frequent visits from human ships that accept passengers. It's an asteroid mining complex that was only recently taken over by humans and the living quarters are very cramped. We stopped there for the first time on our previous circuit, and this time we'll be delivering a police detachment."

"It's dangerous there?" somebody asked.

"There is some crime on the station, but the main problem is claim jumping out in the asteroid belt. Humans originally came to Break Rock to work on a long-term contract for the Frunge, and on its expiration, they leased the facility from the aliens. Unfortunately, the Frunge withdrew their security forces when they left and criminals were quick to take advantage."

"So you're inviting us to stay on the ship for an additional stop?" Nancy asked.

"I've discussed the situation with Flower and she's willing to apply the money already collected for your passage to floor rent at the regular rate. That means for an additional twenty creds each, your cabins will be paid up through the end of the cycle, which gives you almost two months breathing room."

"Does our floor rent include meals?" Jack asked hopefully.

"I'm sorry, but no," Lynx replied. "As somebody who was never enthusiastic about cooking, I can tell you that the ship's cafeterias run by Flower are excellent, and the restaurants that remain open for business while we are in transit between stops are also surprisingly affordable. You'll find that they raise their prices for the tourist trade while we're taking visitors on board."

"You get tourists on a spaceship?" a woman at another table asked.

"It's one of our main functions. In addition to the amusement park and the bazaar, we now have the largest library collection of paper books on or off Earth. Flower complains about the weight causing a minor wobble, though the librarians do distribute the books around the circumference of their section of the deck."

"What happens if we run out of money?" Jack asked. "The rent you're talking about isn't that much different than the fee Shady Oaks was going to charge for management, but I know that some of the people here took a loan to buy into the supposed independent living facility, and whatever income they have left is going to the payments."

"The good news is that there are ample opportunities on board to earn money for anybody willing to work," Lynx replied. "If you can't find a job with a human employer, Flower always has openings for maintaining the ship, and many of those jobs aren't as physically demanding as you might assume."

"Is that an EarthCent uniform?" Irene asked. "It's interesting."

"Flower insists that the ship's officers wear uniforms on official business or she ignores us," Lynx explained. "The Dollnicks are very formal about matters of rank, and as we are all basically guests on board, we've had to make some concessions. Morning calisthenics and the team sport requirement are Flower's policy, not the crew's."

"What about immigration and all that?" Jack asked. "Is there an application process if we decide to remain on board for more than a few weeks?"

"This ship is operating so far below her capacity that we are happy to take on anybody who pulls their weight and behaves themselves," Lynx replied. "Some of you will have pensions or savings that make working on board unnecessary, but in addition to maintaining your physical fitness, there is a community service requirement that can be fulfilled by volunteering."

"That's a lot of interference in our daily lives," Harry said doubtfully. "It doesn't seem right for independent living."

"While I've never set foot in such a facility on Earth, I've read about them in the Galactic Free Press. You'll have far more freedom on Flower, not to mention better food." Lynx paused and took her foot down from the chair. "Listen, I was an independent trader for ten years before I was recruited by EarthCent. For me, freedom meant being on my own ship and answering to no government. Could you say that about your time on Earth?"

"At least they were human rules," Harry said. "We voted in elections, even if it didn't change much. Now you're saying that if we remain here we'll be living by the rules of an alien AI. And how does EarthCent fit into all of this? I know that they have a president on Earth because I've seen him on the news, but what are they doing running a giant space ark?"

"EarthCent is the human government set up by the Stryx when they opened Earth," Lynx explained patiently. "It functions mainly as the point of contact for aliens and their diplomats, and we have embassies on all of the Stryx tunnel network stations with large human populations. We also maintain a presence on a handful of alien worlds that either employ large numbers of humans or attract human tourists, but EarthCent's primary function is diplomatic in nature. The exception is EarthCent Intelligence, which is developing a role in law enforcement for humans who have left Earth. Eccentric Enterprises, the operator of this circuit ship, is an offshoot of EarthCent Intelligence."

"I wish I understood half of that," Harry complained.

"Trust me, it's not important right now. For all of her peculiarities, Flower has been around longer than humanity has practiced agriculture, so she knows more about operating in space than the rest of us put together. She's also in regular contact with the Stryx, who co-sponsor our mission."

"And she's willing to help us?" Irene asked.

"Flower helps those who help themselves," Lynx said. "It's easy for an AI to master languages and build up a library of cultural references, but however human she sounds when you talk with her, remember that she is Dollnick to the core. The Dollys expect everyone to contribute and Flower is no different. My husband is officially the leader of this mission and all of the humans on board, but the ship belongs to Flower—the ship *is* Flower—so if you want to stay here, you'll have to make your peace with that."

"Could you give us until you return tomorrow to decide on our next step?" Nancy asked.

"Of course. This isn't a recruitment drive and you're welcome to stay or to leave at any stop, though again, I would discourage you from getting off at Break Rock. And if you need to reach me at any time, just ask Flower, but don't be surprised if she quizzes you as to the purpose and rejects the request if she doesn't approve. We pay her a fee to act as our switchboard and prevent unnecessary calls."

"Just another minute of your time, please," Jack addressed the gathering after Lynx took her leave. "I'm sure you all noticed that some of my table-mates had more questions than I did, and the third officer will be returning tomorrow, so how about we hold an election now to choose somebody to represent us?"

"You did fine," Harry said.

"But you're the one who just brought up voting in elections!"

"And I pointed out that they didn't make much difference."

"Why don't we ask for a show of hands," Nancy suggested. "All in favor of Jack continuing to represent us through this crisis?"

The only person not to raise a hand was an older man at the next table over.

"Are you interested in the job?" Jack asked the dissenter eagerly.

"No, I'm in favor of you continuing, but my rotator cuff doesn't allow me to raise my hand over my head. Did I hear something about an alien doctor who works cheap? My ears aren't that great either."

"I'll take you by to see the beetle doctor now if you want," Dave offered. "He mentioned that he's open twenty-four hours a day."

"Don't aliens need to sleep?" Harry asked.

"It depends on the species," Nancy said. "Dave told us that the doctor is a Farling, and I read somewhere that they enter a sort of torpor when they aren't active, but they never really sleep. And if you don't mind me tagging along, I think I overdid it shelving books at my volunteer job because my wrist is acting up."

"My neck has been bothering me," an older man said, rising from his chair. "It wouldn't hurt to get a professional opinion."

"This stress over losing our money is upsetting my digestion," a woman added. "Maybe the doctor could give me something."

"I feel like the pied piper," Dave said cheerfully, as half of the retirees lined up behind him to be led to the doctor's office.

"Ask M793qK for a commission," Flower advised him.

Six

"These books I'm carrying right now are from the temporary shelving area behind the circulation desk," Dewey said. "As soon as you've demonstrated that you can shelve books in the proper order, I'll turn you loose on the stacks."

"Like alphabetically?" Julie asked.

"We use a modified version of the Dewey Decimal system."

"It's named after you?"

"Something like that. The main point is the system allows new books to be added to the shelves in the relevant areas without forcing us to reorganize the whole library."

"Why don't you just give them all numbers and be done with it?"

"Because patrons who wish to browse the stacks wouldn't be able to find a section for the Etymology of Classic Latin or for English Maritime Stories. It would all be one big jumble."

"Wait. Everybody is allowed in the stacks *except* for me?"

"You might be tempted to remove a book from the shelf and accidentally put it back in the wrong place. With tens of millions of volumes in the library, a misshelved book is as good as lost."

"But patrons in off the corridor or wherever they come from out here won't make mistakes..."

"They can't. Let me demonstrate." Dewey wheeled closer and presented his shelf of books to the intern. "Pick a book. Any book."

"Now you're doing party tricks?" Julie suspected the AI was making fun of her, but she reached out and pulled a likely looking volume from his shelf. As soon as the book slid free, the remaining volumes came together to close up the empty space.

"All of the library shelves utilize tracked bookends like the ones I just used to push the books together. Patrons are encouraged to place books on shelving carts, but most of them just put the book back in the empty space on the other side of the bookend or lay it on top of the row. The important thing is that we're able to easily identify those books and then shelve them in their proper places."

"So how do we get the bookends to open up?

"The transponder bracelet you were given that identifies you as a library employee unlocks the bookends. Mine is built in, of course." The binocular cameras that served as Dewey's eyes redirected to look over the girl's shoulder. "I believe a patron is approaching."

Julie drew herself up self-consciously and turned to the new arrival. "May I help you?"

"I don't know," the woman replied, eyeing the large 'In Training' badge that hung around the intern's neck. "Just how long have you been working here?"

"Two days, but I can always ask somebody if I can't find what you want."

"My husband and I have staked a Kamacite claim but we don't have much experience in asteroid mining. We recently completed a twenty-year contract on a Frunge mining world."

"Kamacite?"

"It's an iron-nickel alloy, though it's the nickel that makes it valuable. John's more into the technical side of it than I am, but we flipped a coin and I got stuck coming to the library."

"You'd rather be working?"

"My husband is with our kids at the amusement park. If you hurry up, maybe I can get in a couple of rides before it's time for lunch. We bought the family pass."

"Kamacite," Julie spoke at her library-supplied catalog tab, trying to sound confident. She was relieved when the screen filled with book titles and she began scrolling through descriptions. "I'm seeing plenty of references but nothing about mining," she said apologetically.

"They wouldn't have had Kamacite mining on Earth, except maybe from meteorites. I was hoping you'd have a book from one of the other species in translation."

"I think I better ask somebody. Dewey? Could you come over here for a minute?"

The AI rotated his shelving attachment to the vertical in order to reduce the chance of pedestrian accidents and rolled up behind Julie.

"How may I be of service?"

"This patron is interested in books about mining Kamacite but none of the references that came up look promising to me. She wanted to know if we have anything from the other species in translation."

"The library subscribes to the Stryxcat system so we can pull basic technical books from any of the participating species, though only in electronic or holographic form. If you have a storage device, I can select a couple of appropriate titles for you."

"We already have the complete Frunge mining reference set, at least, the techniques they aren't keeping secret," the woman replied. "But other than the pictures it's just too technical for us. John and I don't have a lab to do mass spectrometry or Ramen laser analysis, and we wouldn't know what we were doing anyway. We just want to mine the stuff and sell it."

"I understand," the robot said and turned to Julie. "Has anybody shown you the *For Humans* collection?"

"Bea said something about it being a last resort, but that was all."

"Follow me." Dewey led the intern and the woman to a blank section of bulkhead around the corner from the circulation desk and issued a silent command. A large panel slid aside, revealing hundreds of identically sized paperback books, all sporting gaudy orange spines with *For Humans* prominently spelled out in raised silver foil letters.

"I've seen these before," Julie said. "They were starting to show up in the suborbital airport bookstores before I left."

"Bea insists that we keep *For Humans* books segregated in this section so they don't infect the stacks," Dewey informed them. "The titles are shelved in alphabetical order by the first word in the subject."

"*Mining For Humans*," the woman read off a spine, eagerly pulling out the volume and flipping through the pages. "Oh, this is all about planet-based operations."

"*Asteroid Mining for Humans*," Julie said, pulling a different volume from the top shelf near the far left of the section. She passed the book to the miner, who gave her the other book in exchange. Under Dewey's watchful eyes, the intern carefully returned *Mining For Humans* to its place between *Meteor Screens For Humans* and *Moon Colonies For Humans*.

"This is perfect," the woman said, perusing the step-by-step illustrated instructions with helpful tips and cautions on practically every page. "How much to borrow it?"

"The library doesn't normally charge for loans that are returned on time, but we've found that we need to take a deposit equal to the retail cost for books in this series or we never get them back," Dewey explained.

They returned to the circulation desk where Julie filled out the tab screen to grant the patron a borrower's token. Then the woman passed over a programmable cred, and with help from Dewey, the intern entered the price for the book into the library's Stryx mini-register, which requested the patron's verbal confirmation before debiting the amount from her coin.

"Come again," Julie called after the woman, who had her nose in the book as she headed for the lift tube.

"I'll ping the printer and have him run off another copy," Dewey said. "We won't be getting that one back."

"You order single copies of books?"

"It's all done on-demand just down the corridor. The publisher has a contract with the Galactic Free Press which distributes the source copies of *For Humans* books to authorized printers by way of the Stryxnet."

Dewey headed off to the stacks and Julie practiced sorting returns into the proper order in the temporary shelving area. Then a young man with tattoos of daggers on the backs of his hands stalked aggressively up to the circulation desk. Julie went rigid, certain that this was the end.

"You're it?" he demanded, glaring at her angrily.

"How did you find me so fast?" she asked in a dead voice, though her eyes were busy searching for the most likely escape route.

"The elevator told me where you were," he replied, and his face flushed.

"Lift tube," Flower corrected him from the speaker grille. "He's here for a book, Julie."

"Isn't there a male librarian?" the man demanded.

Julie started breathing again as she sagged in relief. "Just ask me. If I can't help you, I'm sure Dewey can."

"Who's Dewey?"

"Me," the AI said, returning to the circulation desk with an empty shelf ready for a new load. "How can I help you?"

"Make her go away first. It's guy stuff."

Julie stared for a moment before realizing what the patron was talking about, and then she gladly moved to the returns area and continued putting the books in order. Behind her, she had the sense that the man was whispering, though she couldn't actually hear what was being said.

A few minutes later, Dewey rolled up to her side and checked her work. "I believe you have it. I'll inform the rest of the staff that you're authorized for shelving, but to give you fair warning, I'm going to check the locations your bracelet visits and keep an eye on your work for a few days."

"Where did he go? Was he asking for dirty books?"

"Oh, we have plenty of those. The code word is 'adult' and they're down on the left there."

"He must have been in a real hurry," she said, peering down the long passage between the shelves to the point that the deck disappeared in the curvature of the ship.

"No, I sent him to see the doctor. A book isn't going to take care of his problem."

"He has—why did he come to the library?"

"That's what we're here for, to answer questions. You'll get used to people coming in to ask for help with everything in their lives. It's part of our advertising campaign."

"I didn't realize we had one."

"It runs in the localized version of the Galactic Free Press for a whole week before each stop we visit. 'Ask Us Anything – The Library On Flower.' We have ads in the bazaar and at the amusement park as well, and we're looking into placemats for the restaurants."

A tweedy looking man made his way behind the circulation desk and greeted Julie. "I'm Aaron, the second shift head librarian. I can see from the badge that you're our new intern. How do you like it so far?"

"The job is great and the people are nice. Dewey has been teaching me tons."

"I've just authorized her for the stacks," Dewey told Aaron. "There's enough time left on her shift for me to give her the basic tour if you don't need her for anything else."

"Please," the librarian said. He grabbed a book from the returns shelve seemingly at random and settled onto the high stool to read.

"Do you sleep, Dewey?" Julie asked as the robot led her into the stacks.

"I don't see the attraction. For the time being, I work around the clock in the library. Once we get the new additions to the collection all moved in, I intend to take time off for my hobbies. I'm also the only librarian qualified to operate the bookmobile."

"A bookmobile on a spaceship? Are people too lazy to take a lift tube?"

"It's a modified trading vessel not capable of independent jumps, but it's perfect for visiting outlying locations while Flower is at the main population center of a system.

Part of our mission is to establish satellite libraries in human communities that provide a good home for books, and I deliver starter collections. Perhaps you'd like to come along on my next outing."

"How many library collections do you have on board?" Julie asked.

"One hundred and twenty-six, counting the academic libraries. And they're busy packing back on Earth for our next time through. Redeveloping the old library buildings into luxury housing has become a fad in some areas because old structures were usually very sound."

"I never really got the point of paper books on shelves but I've already found two interesting novels that I never would have come across on my tab. The browsing experience is completely different."

"We call it the 'discovery process' in librarian circles, and it is one of the most important functions libraries traditionally served through selective collection building. I understand that the teacher bots actually do something similar with the books they present to young readers."

"With a teacher bot, you could ask questions about anything you didn't understand, discuss the books with groups of other students from all over the world, and learn about the authors and their times."

"It sounds like you have fond memories of your teacher bot."

"I do. It was the happiest part—" Julie cut herself off when she realized she was talking about her childhood and turned away from the AI. "Who's that?"

"Down, Zelda!" Dewey cried. A large black Labrador butted into the intern and then sat down on the girl's feet and leaned heavily against her legs.

"What she doing?" Julie asked.

"Trying to merge with you. Have you met?"

"This is the first time. Is she yours?"

"Zelda considers herself to be part of the library collection but I take care of her food," Dewey said. He reached with a manipulator and began carefully rubbing behind the dog's ears. Zelda's tail started thwacking the deck so hard that it was a wonder to the intern that the dog didn't yelp in pain. "You can borrow her if you're lonely."

Julie had a sudden vision of herself following the large dog around the ship with a scoop and a waste disposal bag and waved off the suggestion. "I'll pass."

"Of course. A pretty girl like you must have to beat them off with a stick."

"Men? It took more than a stick where I grew up." Saying it reminded her that she had fallen out of the habit of carrying a weapon since coming aboard the ship and she made a mental note to see if the bazaar traders had anything she could use for self-defence. "The library seems busier now than it was just a couple days ago," Julie observed as two women entered the public area of the stacks.

"It always takes people a little time to get back to their routines after a long stop at Earth. Which reminds me. We canceled our children's reading hour last week because of the stop but it's back on the schedule today. How about giving it a try?"

"I'm not that bad," Julie said, her ears turning pink. She was sorely aware that the librarians had identified holes in her vocabulary and must have figured out the supposed degree from City College was at best an exaggeration.

"I meant reading to the children."

"I can't risk it. I mean, I shouldn't have children around me. I'm a bit of a disaster magnet."

"That's a shame, I think you'd enjoy it. You should at least come and watch. Maybe you'll change your mind."

"I'm really not comfortable around children," Julie repeated.

"I asked Flower about you," Dewey said quietly. "She wouldn't tell me anything, but I couldn't help putting together the timing of your joining the ship with a certain highly publicized trial that took place on Earth just before we departed."

"I don't know what you're talking about," the girl maintained stubbornly. "Do you want me to shelve the returns?"

"If you let fear control your life than you're letting them win," the AI continued. "I don't know if you've been reading the Galactic Free Press, but every day there's a story about somebody else coming forward to testify against the gangs back on Earth, and they all credit the brave girl who stood up against the syndicate for giving them the courage."

"The brave girl who ran away to space under a fake name," Julie muttered.

"Discretion is the better part of valor," Dewey told her. "If you decide to go public later, we do have a reporter on board."

"Great. So in addition to the captain and Flower, you know who I am."

"Dewey!" the ship's AI interrupted in a thundering voice over a dozen nearby speakers. "Didn't you tell me you wanted to visit the recycling station today?"

"Right," Dewey declared in an artificially cheery tone. "We'll talk later, Julie."

"Why do I get the impression that you're hiding something from me, Flower?" Julie demanded.

"Nothing could be farther from the truth. In fact, if you're up to taking a walk, I've been meaning to show you my reservoir deck."

"Let me just grab my purse from the circulation desk."

"No! I mean, it makes more sense to stop back on your way home than to carry your bag around. Besides, it might get wet. I'm holding the closest lift tube capsule for you. It's in the spoke just down this aisle on the left."

"Is there some hurry?" Julie asked as she entered the lift tube capsule. Flower didn't answer, and when the capsule stopped, the girl added, "I feel a little funny. Like the first time I came aboard."

"You must be more sensitive to minor changes in weight than most of your people," Flower said as the door slid open on a watery wonderland. "A little jogging will help you adjust."

"What?"

"Just take the main radial catwalk out over the lake. Isn't the air nice and cool? Come on, you're wearing sneakers. I've gone easy on you about exercising, you know."

"You said I was off the hook until the theatre team started," Julie grumbled, but she broke into a half-hearted jog. "I have to be at my new waitressing job in a half hour so I can't get all sweaty."

"There's nothing wrong with honest sweat," the AI retorted. "How about some music?"

"What?"

"I'll just pick something."

A chorus of songbirds playing from thousands of speakers blocked out all other sounds as the lift tube doors slid open again behind her. A man carrying a sort of gym bag emerged, and as soon as he spotted the girl jogging away ahead of him, he ran out onto the same catwalk above the swelling water and pulled a crossbow from the bag. Before he could draw a bead on his target, an enormous alien fish that bore a strong resemblance to a shark sailed over the catwalk and took the would-be assassin in its jaws.

Some instinct made Julie stop and look back, even though she hadn't heard the giant splash over the avian cacophony. "What was that?" she shouted, staring at the spreading ripples.

The concert came to an abrupt end, leaving only the gentle lapping of the water to fill the silence. "Nothing," Flower responded. "That's enough jogging for the day. You want to work your way into it gradually."

"Where did that gym bag come from?"

"A fisherman must have left it."

"But I just passed there a minute ago," she said, starting back towards the lift tube. "And why does it look like somebody dropped a giant rock into the lake?"

"Just the fish jumping. You know I'm preserving everything I can for my return to colony ship duty and our large marine life is quite intelligent. No, don't touch the bag. I'll have a bot take care of it.

Seven

"I never would have believed I'd have a disloyal thought about my old two-man trader but I'm getting used to this shuttle," Lynx said to her husband.

"Gig," Flower corrected the third officer over the small ship's comm. "I consulted with one of your librarians and that's the proper term for a craft dedicated to transporting the captain over short distances."

"I'd like it more if my feet reached the deck," Woojin grumbled from the command chair. "I can barely make my toes touch while I'm strapped in."

"I can order you a pair of adjustable high heels from Union Station," the Dollnick AI offered facetiously. "What I won't do is replace that chair with something a real captain wouldn't fit in."

Two men dressed in neat black fatigues sitting in the second row of seats burst out laughing.

"I'm going to miss you, Flower," the younger one said. "It's been a fun couple of months and I've never been in such good shape in my life."

"Oh, don't get her started, Rick," the chief security officer seated next to him groaned.

"I like the stretching myself," Lynx confessed. "At first I wasn't crazy about getting up twenty minutes early and doing group exercises in the corridor, but you get used to it after a few years."

"Woojin?" Flower inquired.

"I hate to admit it, but the exercise is probably good for everybody."

"That's three out of four, Tyrell," the AI informed the security chief. "I couldn't be any more—what do you call it?"

"Sensitive?" Lynx suggested.

"Democratic," Richard said.

"Right," Flower said. "I always have trouble coming up with that word as there's no equivalent in Dollnick. Prepare for deceleration."

The four chairs in the captain's gig swung around to face the rear of the vessel as it approached the Break Rock habitat. The craft slipped through the atmosphere retention field of the docking hub and came to a rapid halt just above an open area of the deck.

"Perfect landing," Flower complimented herself. "Try not to take too long. Missy started brewing a mutiny the moment you entered the gig."

"What?" Woojin demanded in disbelief.

"Did I say mutiny? I meant coffee. Your first officer is always threatening mutiny over the other officers not paying into the coffee fund or cleaning the pot so it's easy to get confused."

"We're trying to make a good impression today so please try not to cause any trouble," the captain admonished the AI as he unbuckled the safety harness and activated his magnetic cleats. "Let's go, people."

The four passengers shuffled down the gig's ramp to be met by an out-of-breath woman holding a sign with 'Eccentric Enterprises' hand-printed in block letters.

"I thought you'd be arriving on one of the shuttle buses or in a taxi," she said, eyeing the advanced Dollnick craft.

"Very impressive. I hope you have some way of securing it. That shuttle is probably worth more than all the other ships docked in the hub combined."

"Gig," Flower's voice echoed through the large space. "And it's worth more than the whole habitat."

"Our ship's AI controls the shuttle," Woojin said, intentionally not using Flower's terminology. "I pity the fool who tries to steal it."

"I see. I'm Annie, official secretary for the Break Rock cooperative. The council members are awaiting your arrival in the War Room."

"You have a war room?" Richard asked. "I thought there was no organized military structure here."

"It's the name of the bar we're using for the meeting," the secretary explained as she led them towards a lift tube. "Habitat space is way too expensive for the council to set up a permanent office. I pretty much run everything from my apartment."

"It's a bit cold, isn't it?" Lynx asked.

"Everybody says that. It's ironic being too cold in space when most artificial structures have trouble getting rid of waste heat. We're leasing the habitat from aliens who programmed the thermostats for their own comfort zone and nobody has been able to figure out how to change them."

"The station doesn't have an AI controller?"

"I guess it didn't want to stay behind with a bunch of humans," Annie replied with a shrug. "Recreation deck," she enunciated for the lift tube controller, and then added for the benefit of the guests, "You have to speak very clearly because English was grafted on to the speech recognition system for us by a couple of hackers. Is one of you our new police chief?"

"Me," Richard said, half raising his hand. "Friends call me Rick."

"I'm afraid you'll have your hands full, Rick. Claim jumping has become a weekly occurrence and miners returning to the habitat have been murdered for their gold. Our volunteer force patrols the family decks, but things can get pretty rough in the transient sections."

"I did notice that the weapons dealers in our bazaar were doing a good business," Lynx interjected.

"Yes. Most of the claims are on isolated asteroids in the belt and the miners can't get insurance coverage unless they go armed. A traveling salesman who came through last month selling life insurance policies said that an unarmed miner is an attractive nuisance, whatever that means."

"I was chosen for this job because I worked security details for a Frunge mining complex a couple of years back," Rick told her. "I'm familiar with the enforcement standards the majority of your people have already experienced."

"I see Eccentric Enterprises has done its homework," Annie said approvingly. "Our original group, myself included, all worked a long-term Frunge contract before accepting a five-year lease on this habitat in lieu of our balloon payment. But after the aliens pulled out, we began attracting all the wrong sorts, and some of us are on the verge of giving up." The lift tube capsule came to a halt, the passengers clicked off their magnetic cleats, and the secretary led them out into a corridor packed with poorly lit bars.

"So this is it for recreation on Break Rock?" Lynx asked,

"There's a section set aside for families that has a few restaurants and a sort of a hydroponic farm, but everybody has always thought of this habitat as a temporary place to make money, not a home. It's why so many parents are interested in enrolling their children in your boarding schools even if the security situation does improve."

A burly man with a shaved head blocked the way with a muscular arm when the secretary attempted to lead her group into the bar.

"Two cred cover," he grunted from his high stool. "Got a D.J. coming on in an hour."

"We're having a meeting," Annie informed him. "I already talked to Nathan and he set aside the back room for us."

"I didn't hear anything about it," the bouncer said, and to illustrate his point, he slid off the stool and moved to body-up against Rick, who was walking next to the council secretary. Two seconds later, he was on his back, thumping his left hand on the floor in submission while the new police chief crouched at his side, holding the bruiser's right wrist at a funny angle.

"I have a good feeling about Rick," Annie commented, as she led the others into the bar.

Behind them, Richard helped the bouncer to his feet and informed him, "New sheriff in town. My door is always open."

"I hope we don't have to wait long for the others," Woojin said, observing that only three council members were present in the back room. "I seem to remember hearing that there are six of you."

"We had a bit of a disagreement over accepting your help," one of the waiting council members said. "Three of our number believe that this is all a trick to bring us under the thumb of some sort of new governmental authority."

"And you don't believe it?"

"Frankly, I don't care, as long as you can stop the claim jumpers. I lost a good friend to those—"

"All right, Carl," Annie interrupted. "We have a lot to get through today and not much time to do it." She set her tab down on the table, tapped something, and said, "Recording."

Nobody seemed to be sure what to do next, so Lynx began by introducing the visitors from Flower.

"I'm Lynx, and I'm the third officer in charge of business operations on Flower. This is my husband, Captain Pyun, our chief of security, Tyrell Hopkins, and your new chief of police, Richard White."

"Rick. And I don't use the last name."

"You'll fit right in here, then," a grey-haired woman said. "I'm the council elder, Linda. That's Carl, and the ugly customer there is Josef. We requested this meeting to discuss the terms Eccentric Enterprises has proposed for our new security force."

"I'm afraid we don't have any flexibility on that account," Woojin told her. "These police deployments are a joint project of Eccentric Enterprises, which is responsible for funding our circuit ship, and the Conference of Sovereign Human Communities, of which you are now a member. Have you discussed this with your CoSHC rep?"

"I'm our CoSHC rep, and I've explained it to these people a million times," Annie said. "The first year of deployment is a proof-of-concept, and the money we kick in won't even cover all of the salaries, not to mention patrol ship leases."

"So you're pulling a bait-and-switch," Josef said angrily, rising to his feet. "The others were right."

"We're trying to create a sustainable infrastructure for humans in space," Woojin said. "We have a police academy on Flower retraining former mercenaries for civil law enforcement, and we'd be happy to accept any candidates from—"

"No, that won't be necessary," Linda cut him off with a wave of her hand. "Josef is just upset because the sum you are proposing is more than we spend on maintenance for the habitat, which is his responsibility."

"I can only wash the air scrubber filters so many times before they start falling apart," Josef grumbled. "What's the use of a police force if we all suffocate?"

"I'm sure that one of the distributors on Flower stocks replacements," Lynx informed him.

"Do you think I don't know that? A Dollnick sales rep has already been here and gone. If I had ten thousand creds to spend I could replace every filter on the habitat, but that Dolly wasn't giving anything away."

"Why should he?" Lynx asked. "I was a trader for ten years and I didn't make a trade unless there was a profit. If you wanted to have all of your needs provided for, you should have signed a second contract with the Frunge. Plenty of groups do."

"Our miners are making plenty of money," Annie said, and from the tone of her voice, it was obvious that she was repeating an old argument. "We're the only member of CoSHC that doesn't have a system in place to raise revenue."

"Give me and my detachment a chance to show your people what we can do and the miners will be knocking down your doors to pay you to keep us on," Richard predicted.

"Confident. I like that. But on the subject of the amount we agreed to pay, we don't exactly have it."

"Excuse me?" Lynx said.

"I mean, we don't have cash up-front."

"Whatever CoSHC negotiated with our home office is the deal and we wouldn't be here if the terms weren't satisfactory," Richard said. "All of our men have a programmable cred supplied by Eccentric Enterprises, and payroll will be handled over the register network."

"Then everything is settled," Annie said, waving the council members into silent acquiescence. "I wish I could offer to cover your men's food and lodging, but we don't directly control any of the resources on Break Rock."

"That's fine, ma'am," Richard told her. "Eccentric already credited everybody in the detachment with move-in expenses and an advance on pay."

"We don't have any equipment for you," Carl spoke up. "Our volunteer police force purchased side arms from traders, mainly stunners, but they only responded to calls inside the habitat. Our real trouble is out in the asteroid belt. One prospector who survived an encounter thanks to a pre-planned escape route reported that the claim jumpers attacked with an armed ship."

"Probably a converted trader," Tyrell said. "Even the smallest alien patrol craft available on the used market are way beyond the budget of most human criminals. Have you seen any indications of Horten pirates getting involved?"

"It's all humans as far as we know," Annie told him. "Some of the finds are big money to us, but by alien standards, the asteroid belt is already played out. The Frunge never would have leased the whole operation to us so cheap otherwise."

"Then we won't have any problems," Richard said. "Our detachment comes with three military-surplus Vergallian Enforcer craft, basically short-range fighters, and each one of those is equipped with two armored spacesuits."

"I've seen those in the immersives," Josef said. "A single soldier wearing that kind of gear could take over this whole habitat and rule as king."

"That's why they're all genetically keyed to the operator so they stay in the right hands."

"We'd hoped to offset most of our share of the cost with prize money," Linda said. "I know how expensive military surplus equipment is because I looked into purchasing some when claim jumping first became a problem. Even the rental on three patrol craft may not be economically justifiable in the long term for the profit our miners are making here."

"The equipment is a loan, it comes from donations," Lynx informed her. "The overall cost is subsidized by Eccentric Enterprises. It's part of a get-tough-on-crime campaign we've undertaken as governments do the same thing on Earth."

"I get it," Annie said. "You don't want the gangs fleeing the crack-downs on Earth getting a toehold out here. Smart."

"Couldn't you just command your colony ship to take care of the problem while you're here?" Josef asked. "Surely an AI from one of the advanced species can sort through all the ships and comm traffic in the system, spot the bad actors, and take them out."

"Flower might agree to clean out this system for a substantial fee but it falls outside of the services we've contracted with her," Lynx explained. "Besides, how long do you think it would take after we left before the next gang of claim jumpers moved in? The whole point of our mission is to help you help yourselves."

"The current gangs are bad enough," Linda told them. "We believe they have undercover members living on the habitat and passing on information. Annie has received death threats."

"Give us a month and you'll be going out to asteroids for picnic lunches," Richard promised her.

Linda insisted on showing Flower's officers the quarters they had arranged for the new police chief and his detachment to rent, and then Woojin, Lynx and Tyrell returned to the gig. Flower began moving before they were finished buckling their safety restraints.

"Late for a party?" Woojin inquired.

"Very funny," the AI replied. "If you'd seen how many Humans tried sneaking aboard while you were off at your meeting you wouldn't be making jokes."

"Why didn't you close the hatch?"

"So you're saying it's my fault some people are desperate to leave Break Rock without paying for passage? And before you claim that your police detachment will turn this place into a paradise by next week, let me tell you what I learned from connecting to their main computer."

"You hacked into Break Rock's systems?"

"I have a responsibility to ensure the safety of my crew and that includes the officers," Flower replied. "I was able to track you and listen in through the habitat's limited systems. Most of the residential space on board is over two-hundred percent capacity with people sleeping in shifts. It's no wonder so many of the parents were willing to register their older children for my boarding schools."

"As long as you've been through their records, are they really as far behind on maintenance as Josef made it sound?" Woojin asked. "I wouldn't want those people suffocating because they can't afford basic replacement parts, and Rick and his men are going to be breathing the same air."

"The Frunge wouldn't have leased the operation to Humans if it really required hands-on maintenance," Flower said grudgingly. "The habitat isn't up to my engineering standards, but not much is. They'll be fine, and Josef will get his filters before we leave. Coming early and starting at a high price is just a standard negotiating tactic for Dollnick sales reps."

"I feel sorry for those people living in such a chilly place," Lynx said, hugging herself reflexively. "Do we have any experts in Frunge interfaces we could send over to help them?"

"I already took care of that," Flower said. "I set the temperature and made adjustments to a number of the creature comfort control systems based on my experience of hosting humans for the last four years."

"Couldn't you have just merged their grafted-on speech recognition with the primary system so they could adjust the temperature themselves?" Woojin asked.

"It's bad for your health to run the temperature up and down like a yoyo all day, which is what would happen if more than one human had access to the controls," the AI explained. "This way, everybody will be happy that it's warmer without making each other miserable trying to get it exactly right."

"You have to admit that Flower's got our number," Tyrell said with a laugh, but then his face turned serious. "We still need to talk about the update from EarthCent

Intelligence that came in right before we left, and this is as good a time as any. The prosecutor's office that handled the trial in which our guest played a starring role has uncovered a leak. We have to assume the syndicate knew that Julie was joining our ship at least twenty-four hours before she arrived, which would have given them more than enough time to send assassins on board."

"I've only identified the one so far," Flower said in a conversational tone.

"There's a contract killer on board and you didn't tell us?" Woojin asked angrily.

"There *was* an assassin on board, but I didn't know who he was until he stalked Julie to the library. Fortunately, he was carrying a variety of weapons which were picked up by the scanner so I was able to put a safe distance between them."

"The library scans patrons for weapons?" Tyrell asked. "I didn't know that."

"Neither do the librarians," the AI replied, sounding a bit smug. "They asked for a system to help prevent book theft, so I had my bots install a basic Dollnick security scanner and I sound a loud buzzer if somebody tries to leave with books that haven't been checked out. They probably assume that's all the equipment is capable of, but I find it useful to sample the level of concealed weaponry people are carrying around."

"Where's the assassin now?" Woojin demanded. "Did he get off at Break Rock?"

"He met with an untimely fishing accident. I'm afraid his body couldn't be recovered, but I'm holding his luggage in storage for your inspection."

Eight

"Thirty-eight suckers," Harry muttered in disgust as he added his written affidavit to the pile on the cafeteria table. "When I get back to Earth, I'm going to sue our real-estate lawyer."

"I wouldn't be hasty," the woman who had volunteered to collect the paperwork admonished him. "I was a practicing attorney for more than thirty-five years and the paperwork we all signed would have fooled anybody. I even insisted on a copy of the hundred-year lease that Shady Oaks claimed to have taken out with the Dollnick clan that built this colony ship, and when I showed it to Flower, she said that if it was real, it would have been in perfect order."

"What does that mean?"

"It means that the people who scammed us were very good at their job. We all made the mistake of rushing for a deal that wouldn't be available again for another six months, and then only at double the price."

"Did you hear that?" Irene asked her husband. "It's not your fault. She's a lawyer and she fell for it too. Besides, even you admit that the food here is terrific. I don't see why we should be in any hurry to return to Earth."

"Stay for the meeting," the lawyer urged Harry. "We're going to talk about forming a cooperative to provide ourselves with all of the services that Shady-whatever promised."

"Sounds like communism," Harry grumbled. "I don't understand why they want me here when I'm skeptical about the whole thing."

"That's exactly why everybody asked you to stay," Irene told her husband. "You can play the devil's advocate."

The common room seemed much larger since maintenance bots had come and removed some of the cafeteria equipment and the surplus tables and chairs that Flower had initially provided to seat a hundred. Only five round tables and forty chairs remained, though the bots had brought in some couch-type furniture that was upholstered in soft alien fabric which had already proved itself to be impervious to spills. The problem was that the new furniture was sized for Dollnicks, and it was difficult for most of the senior citizens to raise themselves high enough to take a seat.

"I'm glad you stayed," Nancy greeted the Blooms when they returned to the table, and she immediately confirmed Irene's guess. "We wanted to include a critical voice on the committee."

"I'm not promising anything," Harry said. "It doesn't make much sense to me that a random group of retired people who had never seen each other up until they got conned out of their life savings should start a new business venture. If anything, I'd think that proves that we're the wrong bunch to try it."

Irene remained on her feet. "I'll see you at home later. I'm going shopping with Lisa at the bazaar to pick up a few things for the cabin."

"Don't forget we're short on cash," her husband called after her.

"How long were you in business?" Nancy asked the baker.

"Practically our whole lives," Harry replied. "I worked in a commercial bakery for a few years after college while Irene was home with the kids, but then her parents told us about the only bakery in their town shutting down because the owners were leaving Earth. They helped us buy the building, and despite what's happened, I'm glad we were able to pass it on to another young couple."

"And everybody else here has a lifetime of experience at something as well. We're all still walking and taking care of ourselves, and remember, if Shady Elms, Oaks, and Pines had been legitimate, the people here are exactly the ones you would have been living with anyway."

"But there would have been professional management," Harry protested. "We may still have most of our marbles today, but what happens in five or ten years?"

"What happens in independent living places back on Earth?" Nancy countered. "As soon as you can't take care of yourself, they move you on to assisted living, or a nursing home. Maybe someday we'll have those options here, but let's deal with one thing at a time."

"Does anybody else want a cup of coffee before a bot takes the urn away?" Jack asked.

"Black, with two sugars," the lawyer replied. "And I'm Brenda, for those of you I haven't met. I counted the affidavits and all thirty-eight of us turned one in, so that completes the information EarthCent Intelligence requested. There's not much else we can do from our end to help the authorities unless they apprehend the perpetrators and want us to testify."

"And now we're going to set up in the same business," Harry said. "All this committee needs is somebody with a background in advertising and we'll be ready to launch our own scam."

"That would be Maureen. She went to her cabin to get something, but—here she is now."

"Hope I didn't keep anybody waiting," a tall woman who didn't look a day over fifty said as she took her seat at the table. "Jack, Brenda, Nancy, myself, and who's the newcomer?"

"Harry. I'm supposed to poke holes in your ideas."

"He was also in business for nearly forty years as a baker with his own shop," Nancy added.

"Excellent," Maureen said, laying a large tablet on the table and swiping it to life. "Is Flower attending our meeting?"

"I'm here," the ship's AI announced through the overhead speaker.

"Two sugars," Jack said, setting a coffee in front of Brenda before taking his seat. "Are you going to record us on that thing?" he asked, pointing at Maureen's tab.

"No. I brought it to show a few things."

"I'm taking notes, it's a habit," the lawyer said, placing a much smaller tab on the table and enabling the recording function. "Ready."

"I'm sure all of us have been talking with Flower about our options this past week, and I know a few people are thinking of taking passage home when we reach a stop with a reasonable space liner connection," Jack began. "Those of us who remain have six months to figure this out before the circuit brings us back to Earth."

"Is six months the limit?" Harry asked. "There's not much point organizing a cooperative or whatever you want to call it if we're just going to fold it again before the year is out."

"It's a question of efficiency. Flower isn't going to throw us off the ship, at least as long as we follow her rules and pay the rent, but she only opened this particular deck to humans because the people who conned us put in a special request for eighty percent gravity and booked a hundred rooms for a trip to Break Rock. If we're going to remain on board after that we'll have to move to one of the residential decks."

"Or, you could find another sixty-two retired humans who want to live with you and you can remain in your cabins," Flower suggested. "One hundred occupants is the minimum number I need to justify housekeeping for a subsection of deck."

"Everybody take a look at this," Maureen requested, turning her tab and tilting it up so that the other four people at the table could see it. "Play," she instructed the device.

A video of smiling senior citizens greeting each other in a large dining hall began to run, and at the same time, an incongruously young female voice asked, "Are you lonely? Having trouble maintaining your home? Do you find yourself eating breakfast cereal for dinner and sleeping through breakfast? You've worked for others all of your life. Isn't it time you did something for yourself?"

"I've seen this," Harry interjected as the music swelled and the meal scene dissolved to be replaced by a hundred well-dressed couples dancing to the music of a live orchestra. "It's—"

"Heavenly Gardens," the voiceover continued. "An independent living community with a difference."

"Here's another one," Maureen said, swiping the final still image off of the screen and instructing the voice interface, "Next up."

"Snow again," grumbled a silver-haired man brandishing a shovel. "I'm getting too old for this." He began clearing the steps of his home, clutched his chest, and toppled to the ground.

A voiceover that could have been ripped from a World War Two educational film for soldiers cut in with, "Men, don't let this happen to you."

The scene shifted to a woman alone in a kitchen, pulling back the foil on a container of gourmet cat food and dumping it onto a saucer. Then she poured herself a cup of tea, spread some of the cat food on a digestive cracker, and took a bite. "Mmm," the woman said. "Tastes like chicken."

"It's six o'clock on Monday evening," a female voiceover announced. "Do you know what your mother is having for dinner? It's time to have *that* talk with your parents. Sunshine Independent Living can help."

"So I chose these two commercials because they represent opposite ends of the spectrum for independent living advertisements currently running on Earth," Maureen said. "The first type of ad is aimed at people our age and offers an idealized image of what we're missing. The other approach is to advertise to family members and convince them that by not moving their parents into a supervised facility they're showing a lack of love."

"Do you have any data as to the effectiveness of the campaigns?" Nancy asked.

"Sunshine Independent Living is now the biggest housing chain on Earth," Maureen said. "They've found a niche repurposing old apartment blocks into secure independent living facilities, and other than the cost and the food, they get pretty good grades."

"I'm a little lost here," Harry said. "Are you talking about all of us choosing a place on Earth and moving there together if we ever get our money back?"

"I forgot you weren't at our first informal meeting," Jack said. "None of us expect our money to be returned, but it's possible we might be able to earn it back."

"Working odd jobs for Flower?"

"By operating our own independent living business. Why should all of the profits go to people who live in condo towers or mansions? You keep bringing up professional management, but what if we supply the management ourselves?"

"But it can't be as simple as making our own commercials and getting new people to sign up," Harry objected immediately. "There's a lot to providing a home and meals for a large group of people, and I know something about the latter..."

"Exactly," Nancy said as he trailed off. "I've spent much of the last week thinking about what convinced me it was time to leave my home and move to an independent living facility and I realized that Flower already provides the majority of services I need. The hardest part for most people our age is taking care of our property and feeding ourselves, and you've already admitted that the food here is wonderful."

"What was anybody offering in those commercials that isn't better and cheaper here?" Maureen asked. "We have access to the agricultural decks, some of which are nicer than any park I've ever visited. And the opportunities here for a social life beat any of the independent living facilities I looked into before signing up with Shady Oaks. In addition to each other, it's only a two-minute lift tube ride to all of the attractions a city would have to offer, and that doesn't even count the fact that Flower is always available to chat."

"How about the dance?" Harry said stubbornly. "I doubt there's an orchestra on this ship."

"And I doubt there's an orchestra at any independent living complex on Earth unless it's made up of the inmates."

"They aren't inmates, Maureen," Jack said. "Flower? Are there any orchestras on board?"

"Several, though I think a quartet or quintet would be more suitable for any dances you put on in this room. And if anybody is worried about living alone, for a small additional fee I can monitor your physical activity and send a bot to check if you stop moving for too long."

"You actually want a bunch of old humans living on your ship?"

"As long as they follow the rules and pay their bills, I'd happily host a million more just like you," the ship's AI replied. "Did you think that Dollnicks never age?"

"I hadn't given it any thought," Harry admitted. "Besides, I can't imagine that you were in the business of transporting geriatric colonists."

"Actually, she was," Nancy told him. "I've been reading up on Dollnick colony ships and it turns out they transplanted entire communities, babies, old folks, livestock and all. They've been a spacefaring species for millions of years so they aren't exactly roughing it."

"The way I see it, getting scammed should bring us plenty of free publicity if we play our cards right," Maureen said. "We should start by getting in touch with the Galactic Free Press and offering them our story, which will also help prevent the crooks who conned us from going somewhere else with a human population and repeating the same trick. Once we build public awareness of what happened, we hit them with a documentary about our triumphant journey to building a new independent living community in space."

"I don't want to be in a documentary that shows me struggling to touch my toes during our morning torture session in the corridor," Harry objected.

"How much lower can you reach than when you first arrived?" Jack asked.

"That's not the point."

"Have you chosen a sport yet?" Nancy inquired.

"Irene talked me into signing up for the theatre team," Harry said. "Apparently we don't meet while the ship is stopped because everybody is too busy making money off the visitors."

"So you can brush up on your acting chops for our documentary," Maureen said. "I'd also like to make some short videos about life here to send to our families and friends, and if we get lucky, maybe something will go viral."

"We should break down the tasks ahead of us and form mission groups," Jack suggested. "When I contracted on Dolly ag worlds their management style was to assign quotas and schedules and then to leave us to come up with our own strategies for doing the job."

"My wife would probably be willing to shoot video, though she'll need equipment," Harry said.

"I can work with her, and also handle public relations through the press," Maureen said. "You know, after my parents retired, I remember them attending all sorts of adult education or continued learning courses, including some at the local college. I wonder if we could offer something like that. Nancy?"

"The library has an excellent lecture series, and I can rough out some plans for setting up our own classes if we can get enough people to join." The former teacher's eyes practically lit up at the possibilities. "Oh, I don't think I'll be able to sleep tonight because I'm so excited."

"Jack has already asked me to look into any legal requirements," Brenda said. "Flower may not care about human laws, but we also have to deal with Eccentric Enterprises, since they and EarthCent are the closest thing to a government out here. And we'll need to come up with some cost estimates to determine how much we'll have to charge to make this work. Could you handle the food services, Harry?"

"You mean, manage them?" the retired baker asked.

"Just work with Flower to come up with cost estimates for now. Maybe she'd be willing to give you a tour of her kitchen facilities and the supply chain so we'll have some facts to put in our brochure."

"I do want to see her bakery in action," Harry admitted. "Alright, but this doesn't mean I'm in favor of the whole plan. What are you going to work on, Jack?"

"I've tasked myself with talking to everybody who signed up with us and learning about their financial situation, assuming that they're willing to share the information. Our first responsibility has to be to the group that's already here, and if we can't make this thing work for us, I don't want to scale up our problems. We have six months to put our house in order so none of us need feel any pressure."

An older man carrying a large rucksack entered the common room, looked around, and asked, "Am I too late for supper?"

"Lift tube is just down the corridor on the right," Harry told him. "You must have gotten off on the wrong deck."

"This isn't the new independent living community? I had a lucky strike on Break Rock, and at seventy-four years old, I'm hanging up my shovel. I'm not interested in going back to Earth so I was planning to try life on one of the Stryx stations or an open world. Then your ship's AI told me there's an opportunity to get in on the ground floor of a new cooperative here. I hope I'm not too late to buy in."

"So much for six months," Jack said. "What's your name?"

"Boris."

"Why don't we get you squared away with a cabin and then I can take you down to the food court. Flower?"

"Deck 17, Corridor 3, Cabin 65," the Dollnick AI replied through an overhead speaker. "Everything is prepared."

"I may as well take you," Harry offered the newcomer. "Our cabin is right next to yours and I've been meaning to check out the food court. I hear there's a pretty good diner."

"I'm Nancy," the former schoolteacher introduced herself. "That's Harry, Jack, Brenda, and Maureen. We manage the independent living facility."

"And you chose to live here too?" Boris asked, obviously impressed. "I'm beginning to see I made the right decision."

Nine

As soon as she finished her four-hour library shift, Julie headed for the deck where the bazaar shared space with an amusement park and a maze of food stalls. She'd only been on the giant ship for a week, but she already felt like an old hand compared to the visitors from Break Rock, and she was looking forward to her first full shift waitressing. Hank, the owner's son, was working the counter at *The Spoon* when she arrived. He greeted her with a groan of relief.

"I was beginning to worry that Mom was just pulling my leg about hiring you after your tryout," the teenager said, sliding two plates onto the tray at the waitress station. "The specials are for the couple with all the bags at table six."

Julie went right to work, balancing the tray at shoulder height and heading for the customers Hank had indicated.

"Table service," the female of the couple commented with a smile. "I didn't realize we'd come to such a classy diner."

"It looks like you've had a successful outing," Julie said, transferring the plates to their table.

"I bought every season of 'Galactic Core Wars,' for just twenty creds," the man boasted. "The Vergallians have been producing it for hundreds of years. I'll never need to leave our cabin again!"

The woman, his wife or girlfriend, shook her head and shared a knowing look with the waitress.

"Are they subtitled?" Julie asked.

"What? No, my implant does Vergallian, of course," the man replied. "Besides, I've been watching their dramas for so long that I probably know enough to get by."

"Do you remember what happened when you tried ordering a drink in that Vergallian bar on Echo Station?" the woman teased him.

"Well, that was almost five years ago, and the med bot fixed me right up."

"Can I get you anything else?" Julie asked, watching out of the corner of her eye as a pair of middle-aged women visiting from Break Rock took one of the open tables.

"We're all set, thanks."

Julie returned to the waitress station and grabbed a couple of menus, pausing to wipe what she hoped was a trace of ketchup off one of them. Then she leaned over the counter to the ice machine and filled a small metal scoop, the contents of which she split between two clean glasses and topped with water. She caught Hank looking in her direction and used her thumb and forefinger to push up the corners of her mouth into a professional smile. The teen's look of appreciation turned the smile genuine.

"Is this your first time at *The Spoon*?" she asked the women, not expecting an answer since the question was so patently ludicrous. "The menus are just a guideline. Our chef is happy to accept custom orders."

"Are you calling that boy a chef?" one of the women asked skeptically, peering at the counter.

"Food is his life."

"Do you really have fresh eggs?" the other woman demanded, pointing to the claim at the top of the menu. "They aren't reconstituted from powder or that weird liquid stuff?"

Julie whistled sharply, and when Hank turned to see what was up, she drew in her elbows and made little flapping motions with her hands. The teen laughed and held up a glass bowl full of brown eggs for the women to see before he returned to slicing vegetables.

"All of the food we serve is fresh," Julie informed the ladies, and proceeded to decant a bit of the information that Hank's mother had poured into her during her trial shift. "The ag deck farmers make deliveries several times a day when we're busy."

The women tried not to look impressed but failed. Practically all of the food available on the Break Rock complex was synthesized or imported, most of it dehydrated or canned.

"Maybe I'll try the Venus omelet, hold the onions," the first woman said after studying the menu. "Don't waste time, Beth. This ship is leaving in a few hours and I want to get some more shopping in."

"I'll have the salad with farmer's cheese," Beth decided and ran her finger down the beverages list. "Plus a glass of orange juice."

"You have orchards on the ship?" the first woman asked, turning back to the menu.

"That's what they tell me, but I haven't had a chance to visit them yet," Julie replied. "I'll put your order right in."

Customers and orders came and went at a steady pace until the rush finally passed and she was able to sit at the counter to indulge in a coffee with the short-order cook.

"Can you cover for me a minute while I run to the bathroom?" he asked.

"Sure. Where is it, anyway?"

"Sternward, before the next spoke on the left. That way," he added when the girl looked at him blankly. "Flower didn't swap out all of the toilets for human use so don't be surprised by anything you see in there."

"Got it," the girl said. The cook had only been gone a few seconds when a new customer approached, a member of one of the tunnel network's older and wealthier species who happened to resemble enormous bunnies with kangaroo pouches. A pair of Grenouthians worked in the bazaar selling immersive dramas in the entertainment section, but she couldn't tell whether the bunny tapping its furry foot and looking impatient was one of them.

"Can I help you?" Julie asked. She hadn't had the opportunity to speak with any aliens yet, and lacking an implant of her own, she hoped that the bunny would have a method of communicating.

"Do you have a container that will keep salad fresh?" a translation pendant worn on the Grenouthian's necklace squawked at her in a tinny voice.

"Of course. But this is a diner and we sell—"

The Grenouthian cut her off with a dismissive wave of a giant paw and repeated, "Do you have a container that will keep salad fresh?"

Unsure of what the big alien was after and tired from her long day, Julie shot back with, "You'll have to speak slower. I'm human."

The Grenouthian relaxed visibly and drew a small leather bag from his pouch which he passed to Julie. The weight of the bag surprised her, and it slipped out of her hand to fall on the counter where it landed with a muffled clink of shifting coins. As the bunny looked on disdainfully, she peeked inside and gasped at the gold pieces featuring a furry head in profile.

"You'll find that it's all there," the Grenouthian continued. "Give me what I came for and I'll be in touch with instructions before the next stop."

"Do you want a menu?"

"Don't play games with me, Human."

"I don't know what you want. Are you trying to buy the diner? I'm sure this gold is enough to cover the cost, but I'm not one of the owners."

"Who are you?" the Grenouthian demanded.

"I'm Julie. I work here."

"Impossible, she knew the countersign," the bunny muttered to himself. "Give back that gold."

"I thought you said you wanted a salad," she said, passing back the bag.

"Idiot!" the Grenouthian grunted, then turned on his heel and stalked away.

"Uh, Flower?" Julie asked, not directing her voice anywhere in particular.

"Yes," the ship's AI responded from a speaker above the refrigerator.

"Why did a giant bunny just offer me a bag of gold and then take it back?"

"I can think of several explanations but they would be pure speculation on my part."

"I can't think of any explanations and I don't like it. Would you mind sharing one of yours?"

"Mistaken identity ranks high on the list. I couldn't help overhearing your exchange with the Grenouthian and I suspect you passed his challenge query when you asked him to speak slower."

"So who am I supposed to look like? Do I have a doppelganger running around the ship working for some kind of bunny mafia?"

"The general rule when you're dealing with other species is that the less you look like them, the more they think you all look alike."

"Oh, I guess that makes sense."

"Did I miss something?" Hank asked, coming back behind the counter and drying his hands on a towel. "I don't like the infrared dryers in the bathroom," he added by way of explanation. "My skin gets dried out enough from scrubbing pots and pans."

"A Grenouthian came in and offered me a bag of gold," Julie said and stared at the young man suspiciously. "Are you selling drugs out of this place?"

"Not me, and my folks would never go along with anything illegal. What did the bunny say?"

"He asked me if I had a container that would keep salad fresh, then he handed over a bag of gold and said to give him what he came for and that he'd have instructions for me later. When I told him that I work here, he called me an idiot and took back the gold."

"Maybe he was expecting to meet a customer. You were sitting at the counter and you say he left when you told him you worked here."

"That must be it. Sorry for accusing you like that."

"Heads up," Hank said and busied himself scraping the grill.

Julie turned and saw that an elegantly dressed woman had come into the service area and taken the table farthest from the counter. She grabbed a menu and a glass of ice water and went to greet the customer.

"Breakfast anytime?" the woman asked.

"Everything on the menu anytime," Julie assured her. "Can I start you off with a cup of coffee?"

"Herbal tea if you have it. Mint."

"Can do. I'll be back with it in a jiff."

"Waitress," the customer addressed her as she was turning away. "Do you have the time? I'm supposed to meet somebody but I'm afraid I forgot to update my implant with the ship's clock when I came aboard after transferring at Break Rock."

"I can't afford an implant and I don't have a tab with me," Julie said apologetically. "I'll check with the cook." She returned to the counter and asked Hank for the time while drawing a cup of hot water and retrieving a bag of mint tea from the herbal assortment on display.

"Flower. What time is it?" the cook asked.

"Time for you to buy an implant or a watch," the AI replied irritably. "I'm going to start charging per word if you keep wasting my time with dumb questions. It's eighty-one past the hour."

Hank grimaced and said, "I can't translate from Dollnick time, Flower. It's for Julie. A customer asked her."

"I know that. The time on your bifurcated scale that doesn't even accurately represent the length of a solar day for your planet is nine thirty-two post meridiem."

"Thank you, Flower," Julie said and returned to her lone customer with the tea. "It's nine thirty-two in the evening."

"Oops," the woman said, slumping in her seat. "Did you happen to see a Grenouthian earlier? I'm sure you can't get too many of them."

"You just missed him."

"Oh, no! Now I'll have to hunt him up and their residential areas are always a maze." She put down the menu, looked at the tea, and asked, "Do you have anything stronger? Like vodka, maybe?"

"I can ask," Julie said, and going behind the counter, whispered to Hank, "It's her, the woman the bunny was looking for. What do I do?"

"Does she want anything from you?" the cook asked.

"Vodka. We don't have an alcohol license, do we?"

Hank gave her a look. "You really are a greenhorn. You don't need a special license to sell booze on the ship and we keep some local stuff at the back of the fridge for our regular customers. It's just that nobody would come here to sit down and have a drink."

Julie checked behind the bottles of milk and juice, and sure enough, she located a bottle crudely labeled 'Deck Three Vodka.' She added an empty juice glass to the tray and brought it out to the customer with an apologetic shrug.

"Deck Three Vodka?"

"Maybe you want to take a little taste before committing," Julie said. "I don't even know what we charge since it's not on the menu."

"Not very much would be my guess," the woman said, nodding for the waitress to pour a sample. "So you're new in the job. Have you been aboard Flower long?"

"A while," Julie replied cautiously. "If there's nothing else…"

The woman gulped the sample, coughed, and said, "Could be worse. Pour me a double. Would you have time to sit for a minute?"

Julie felt herself stiffening with suspicion, but the customer was delicately made, more of a femme fatale type than a syndicate assassin, and it would be awkward turning her down when there were no other customers to serve. She settled into the open chair, but her legs were tense, and after pouring a stiff drink, she kept the bottle on her side of the table so it wouldn't be available to the other woman as an improvised weapon. "Julie," she introduced herself stiffly.

"Gina," the woman replied and drank half of her vodka in one go. "I'm sorry to impose on you like this but I've been traveling for weeks and I barely know which way is up."

"You look well rested," Julie couldn't help observing.

"I was in stasis for the last leg of the trip on the Gurch. We just arrived at Break Rock a couple hours ago and I set my wake-up call for when transportation to Flower was available."

"The Gurch?"

"A Frunge liner. My employers wanted me to rendezvous with my contact on Flower as soon as possible but I couldn't find any ships to Earth from—where I was," Gina concluded after a pause.

Julie gave a mental shrug and decided to be blunt. "A giant bunny approached me right before you came and tried to give me a bag of gold."

To Julie's surprise, Gina burst out laughing and couldn't stop herself. When she regained control after several attempts, she quickly knocked back the remainder of her vodka, coughed again, and slapped the table.

"That's the funniest thing I've ever heard. He's going to be furious with himself. Do you have a surveillance camera here? I'll pay you for the video."

"Uh, I don't know," Julie said and called over to Hank. "Do we have a security camera here?"

"Not us. Flower may have something. Flower?"

"Just infrared imaging in your area," the AI replied. "You wouldn't find it very interesting, but your griddle is running a bit cold."

"Thanks."

"That's a shame, but I suppose it's best for operational security," Gina said. "Oh, fudge, forget I said that. I'm just not very good at this cloak-and-dagger stuff." She looked at her empty vodka glass and added, "I probably shouldn't drink, but give me another one."

Against her better judgment, Julie poured her customer another drink, but when she rose shortly afterward to get menus for two new arrivals, she took the bottle with her and returned it to the fridge.

"Just coffee for us, Julie," the smaller woman called to her. "No need to bring menus."

The waitress looked again and saw that the petite woman who had been half-hidden by her companion when she entered was one of the library volunteers who helped in the children's reading program.

"Hi, Nancy," Julie greeted her, bringing over two mugs of coffee with creamers and sugar so the women could mix their own. "You look like you just had an adventure."

"We took the shuttle transport over to Break Rock just to see what a mining habitat is like," the other woman said. "I'm Irene."

"Are you also from the independent living cooperative Nancy was telling me about?"

"Yes, my husband and I were the last to join, I think. He and I ate lunch here a couple of days ago. Harry has always been a big diner fan."

"So what was it like on Break Rock?"

"I'll put it this way. I'm glad I'm back."

"The air smelled a little funny and everything was built on a much smaller scale," Nancy said. "The curvature of the decks made me feel like I was walking in a squirrel cage, and to be totally honest, it wasn't very clean."

"I wouldn't say it was unsanitary," Irene added. "Just run down. We were only there for two hours because almost all of the space is either residential or industrial, though we did get to tour the ore processing facility."

The two older women exchanged a laugh.

"What's so funny?" Julie asked.

"I think it would be impossible to visit the Break Rock habitat and not tour the ore processing facility since it takes up almost all of the space on the inner decks," Nancy said. "We're both a little old to be hanging out in bars with miners, so we hired a young girl to show us around the hydroponic garden. I never realized how many tomatoes could grow on a single vine, and it seemed to be their only crop. So how is the part-time job treating you?"

"I like it. I offered to work a double shift because apparently nobody comes in during jumps and I'd rather be awake than have another nightmare."

"Didn't you work at the library today?"

"Yes, but just four hours. And I haven't started my team sport yet so the time kind of drags for me."

"There must be plenty of young people your age on board," Nancy scolded her. "You should be going out and having fun."

"I'm still adjusting," Julie replied. As soon as she said it, she realized that living around people who weren't all drug pushers or addicts really was more of a change than she had expected.

"What's your team sport?" Irene asked.

"Theatre. I've never been in a play before and I'm kind of nervous, but Flower guaranteed that it was the best match for me, and it's not like I played any sports back on Earth."

"My husband and I are signed up for theatre as well. I wonder if there's more than one group?"

"I think Flower said that the Grenouthian who runs the theatre starts a new team for every production but he can only handle one group of amateurs at a time. I guess we'll be seeing each other."

Ten

"Attention all shoppers. We will be departing the Break Rock asteroid mining complex in five minutes. Visitors who fail to disembark on time will be charged the cost of passage to our next destination at commercial rates and be subject to ship's law. This is your final warning."

Woojin did a standard hand slash under his throat to tell Flower to close the comm, and then he watched the main viewer as the heat signatures from a few stragglers bobbed across the docking bay for the last transportation back to the mining station habitat.

Exactly five minutes passed before the ship's AI informed him, "Starting main engine sequence. We will be in the clear to jump in one hour and twelve minutes." There was a brief pause before Flower continued, "Seconds not reported, as per your request."

The captain looked down at his coffee and watched it slosh gently in the direction of the giant colony ship's stern as Dollnick engines created forward acceleration. Flower did a masterful job of managing the thrust so that only the most sensitive inhabitants would even notice that they were getting underway.

Woojin drained his coffee and returned the mug to the drying rack over the small sink without washing it. "I'll head up to the food court and have a look around. That's where the stowaways always seem to hide."

"Because I don't grant access to the residential decks to anybody whose voice I don't recognize," Flower reminded him. "I'll scan for thermal signatures and ping your implant to let you know if there are any obvious oddities."

Woojin exited the bridge and entered the lift tube across the corridor. "Amusement park deck. Food court," he announced, even though the ship already knew where he was going. The capsule immediately began accelerating outward from the technical deck which was built around the primary engines, jump drive, and a docking bay, all distributed along Flower's axis. When the capsule halted and the door slid open, he paused for a few seconds to let his body adjust before exiting. Moving away from the ship's core had increased his weight from a fraction of Earth standard on the bridge to almost normal.

"Hey, Cap," a tall alien greeted him. The Dollnick was putting away silverware with one hand, wiping down the counter with another, and stacking creds with a third. He used his fourth hand to give the human a casual wave. "Not a great turnout this stop, though I hear the distributors had a field day selling replacement parts for the habitat and new mining equipment to prospectors."

Woojin's implant translated the Dollnick's bird-like trills and whistles seamlessly into English, and he replied, "That's not surprising, Lume. There must be over a hundred thousand humans in this system for the gold rush and many of them arrived unprepared. The amazing thing is just how much equipment the distributors keep in stock."

"It's not like Flower has any capacity constraints," the alien responded, his own implant translating Woojin's speech. "My friend's hatchlings claim that decks four through twelve are haunted, and his wives encourage the belief to keep them from getting lost."

"Humans think that deck forty-three is haunted as well," Woojin jested, since it was inhabited by Dollnicks who found their weight on that deck perfect for sleeping. "Speaking of humans, have you noticed anybody staying behind?"

Lume motioned Woojin closer with his free hand and then indicated the recycling area with a nod. "I saw a suspicious looking youngster head that way just after your final departure warning. Going by his clothes, I'd say he's been living rough somewhere."

"Thanks." Woojin squared his shoulders and walked reluctantly towards the screened-off area where the recycling bins were located. Confronting stowaways was one of the more unpleasant aspects of his job. Most of them were underage kids who were running away from home, and some had even risked their lives in an elevator container from Earth, not knowing if the air would hold out long enough for them to reach the hub. Woojin approached quietly and heard the telltale sounds of somebody foraging through the bins. He managed an artificial cough to announce his presence as he stepped through the entrance.

A figure whose upper body was invisible in the depths of a compost bin froze like a small mammal hoping to escape the attention of a predator. "Are you all right?" the captain asked, coming to a halt at a safe distance. "Did you, uh, lose something?"

The head and torso that reluctantly emerged from the bin proved to belong to a young man, so the Dollnick had gotten that much right. Woojin would have recognized the starved look in the kid's eyes even if he hadn't caught him digging through the compost for a meal. The stowaway appeared to be in his late teens or early twenties, but he had the appearance of somebody who had been burning the candle at both ends for some time, making it hard to be sure about his age. Taut skin stretched across too-prominent cheekbones, and his clothes had an unmistakably lived-in look and smell.

"Who are you?" the kid demanded roughly.

Woojin frowned, wondering why he tried to be polite. "I'm the captain," he replied stiffly. "Did you think I'm wearing this uniform because I want to lead a parade?"

"Oh." The kid kept one hand hidden behind his back, but other than that small gesture of defiance, his tough-guy pose wilted into something more like exhaustion.

Woojin kept both of his own hands close to his body, the fingers spread with his palms towards the kid in what he hoped would be perceived as a non-threatening display.

"Do you mind showing me what's behind your back?"

The stowaway hesitated a moment, then he brought out a half-eaten vegetable-wrap, his face turning as red as the protruding slice of tomato. His hand shook badly and his voice wasn't much steadier. "I'm really hungry, sir, and all of the restaurants are closed."

"My name is Woojin, and if you eat that Drazen fire roll you'll never be hungry again. What's your name, son?"

"Bill," the boy replied, staring at his intended meal with a newly tragic expression. "Are you sure?"

"About the fire roll? Oh, you must have thought that was an Earth tomato. I take it you haven't lived much around aliens."

"I only left Earth with the picker crew eleven months ago and they kept us together at all times. The labor contractor lied about everything," he added angrily, standing a little straighter. "It was like being an indentured servant, only there was no way to save enough money to get out. I stowed away on a supply ship for Break Rock, but the only people there willing to give work to a stranger turned out to be in gangs."

Bill clamped his lips shut after making that statement, apparently realizing that he had just confessed to being a double-fugitive, but Woojin was already feeling better about the latest addition to the ship's population. Alien labor agencies recruiting human workers had to abide by the rules of the ancient race of artificial intelligence that had opened Earth, but human contractors weren't subject to the same regulations, and abuses were common.

"I'm not running a police state here," Woojin informed him. "You're on the good ship Flower operating under a lease arrangement to Eccentric Enterprises. If you have any incriminating information about your former employers, we're the closest thing to a police force humanity has going out here."

Bill seemed to be having a hard time figuring out what to say next, so Woojin decided to help him finish his story. "So you ditched the crooks and stowed away on my ship."

"I still don't understand why nobody on Break Rock would hire me. I was willing to work for food."

"You just showed up at the wrong place at the wrong time," the captain informed him. "Prospectors were turning up dead and the group who leased the complex from the aliens couldn't trust outsiders."

"Well, they almost made me into what they feared. When the guy the gang assigned to show me the ropes gave me a stunner and explained what they did, I shot him, took his money, and grabbed the next transport for your ship. I hid out under the merry-go-round for thirty-six hours and I was afraid to come out to buy something to eat."

"Drop that fire roll in the bin and we'll find you a meal that won't burn holes in your stomach," Woojin told him, amused by the way the kid had turned the tables on the gang. "You give your information to our security chief, Tyrell, and I'll grant you transient status and add your name to the manifest. If you can't find enough paying jobs to make your floor-rent, there's always work helping the ship's bots."

"Floor rent?"

"As big as she is, Flower is a private ship, and everybody aboard has to pay in to keep her running. Even though we're way under capacity for population the overhead costs are enormous. It's a good group of people, though, and we had representatives of seven species on board at last count. Do you have an implant?"

"I couldn't afford anything like that."

"I'll loan you an old ear-cuff translator from ship's stores," Woojin continued, leading the kid into the restaurant section. "They can't do noise cancellation so you'll be hearing the translation at the same time as the source, but maybe you'll pick up a few alien words that way."

After a long hesitation, Bill finally replied, "Thank you," and the pause told Woojin as much about the kid as the brief history he had recounted. "I have a little money, but when I came out of hiding, everything was closed.

"Most of these places are set up to operate when we have visitors, but there are a couple of diners open around the clock for the ship's complement. Is that a permanent limp you have there?"

"Gang initiation. I had to fight six guys and they beat me up pretty good."

"You'll be relieved to hear that we don't have any gangs on this ship, though you'll have to join a sports team if you stay on board." Woojin steered the young man confidently through the narrow passages between the food stalls, an arrangement intended to help create a festive impression when crowds were modest. The walk ended with an obstacle course of empty tables scattered in an open area in front of a long counter. "Take a seat. You must be starving."

"Where is everybody?" Bill asked, climbing stiffly onto the stool.

Woojin slapped the silver bell on the counter several times. "They're open around the clock so the cook has probably just stepped out for a minute. He lifted the glass bell cover off an old-fashioned pastry stand. "Have a muffin to get started."

"Limited menu," Julie told the customers waiting at the counter when she returned from the bathroom. "Sorry, I was just, uh, stretching my legs. The owner asked me to cover for a couple of hours while everybody is home sleeping through the jump."

"Anything will be fine," Woojin told her, and the young woman slipped behind the counter and tied on an apron.

"I'm Julie," she introduced herself. "I can make eggs or burgers, but other than that, you're probably better off sticking with wrapped sandwiches from the fridge. What's with the costume?"

"It's his uniform," Bill told the waitress. "He's the captain."

"Sorry. Am I in trouble now?"

"Not with me," Woojin said. "I'll have a coffee to go with this blueberry muffin plus whatever Bill here is having.

"Got it. What can I get you?" she asked, turning her attention to the young man.

"Eggs, any kind, and toast. Can you make pancakes?"

"Scrambled eggs and toast, and pancakes if there's pre-made mix in the fridge. Do you want a coffee?"

"Better have something with less bite until you get some food in your stomach," Woojin told the young man. "Try the fresh milk."

"You have cows on this ship?" Bill asked skeptically.

"It's a colony ship, isn't it?" Julie replied as if she had grown up on board. "We have two dairy co-ops, a brewery, and I don't know how many farms."

"Over two hundred if you include the aliens, but they're mainly small family operations," Woojin informed them. "Flower also maintains an agricultural base for us herself, but she encourages private enterprise in the Dollnick tradition." He noted Bill's look of surprise and added, "You can always get work on one of Flower's ag decks."

Julie broke open the eggs for Bill's order and began beating them with a whisk. "I didn't see any pancake mix so I'm giving you four eggs. You look hungry." Then she turned her back on the men to brush some butter onto the griddle top and pour out the beaten eggs.

Woojin reached over the counter, lifted the coffee pot from its hotplate, grabbed a cup and saucer from the rack of clean dishes that hadn't been put away yet, and poured himself a cup.

"Help yourself, Captain," Julie added without turning around. "Will that be white toast or wheat?"

"White, I guess," Bill said. "I don't remember the last time anybody asked me what I wanted to eat."

Woojin took a swallow of hot coffee to get the muffin crumbs out of his throat and launched into a little orientation talk for the young man.

"Our mission is sponsored by Eccentric Enterprises, which operates as a sort of subsidiary of EarthCent, though the Stryx are covering a good portion of our fixed expenses for reasons of their own. We're out here to provide support to independent human communities, mainly people who have completed long-term labor contracts for one of the alien species and don't want to return to Earth."

"So you're like a charity?" Bill asked.

"Farthest thing from it. We charge for all of our services and the goal is to run at a profit, though we have some wiggle room from our financial backers when it comes to things like providing police support. There's no such thing as a free lunch, I mean, aside from the one you're eating now." He stopped talking and pointed at his own head.

"Is something wrong with your ear?" Julie asked, and when Woojin didn't reply immediately, she got Bill's attention and mouthed, "Is he really the captain?"

"Sorry," Woojin said. "I have an implant for communications and translation, and pointing at your ear is the usual way of telling people you have an incoming ping."

"So?" Julie asked.

"Ship's business." He rose and placed a ten cred coin on the counter, enough to pay for two good dinners. "Keep the change. Bill, I've asked the ship's AI to find you an open cabin. Just get on any lift tube and ask for 'Bill's room,' and she'll guide you there. Don't be surprised if Tyrell comes by first thing in the morning to debrief you. He's an early riser."

"Thank you," the young people chorused as Woojin strode away from the diner.

As soon as the captain was around the corner he broke into a jog. "You're sure about this, Flower?" he subvoced for his implant pick-up.

"The individual walked right through one of the areas where I have a high-resolution camera on his way to the lift tube. His facial tattooing definitely matched a list of known assassins supplied to me by the Stryx. He's a human renegade who's spent fifteen years with Horten pirates."

"Armed?"

"Even a naked assassin is a threat, but he's carrying a variety of weapons."

"And he's heading this way?"

"Yes, and his heat signature is identical to the one I saw at the library when I heard somebody asking about the new intern. I need to tell Dewey not to be so helpful." The AI paused a moment, and then added, almost apologetically, "I intend to move some cameras back into the docking area before our next stop so I can screen visitors before things get this far. I suppose I can mount a few in the library as well. I'll tell them it's for theft deterrence."

"How come you don't have cameras all over?"

"My last crew insisted on more privacy and we arrived at a compromise number. I deployed most of my remaining cameras where I could watch the children."

Woojin came to a halt as soon as he could see the lift tube he had arrived in ten minutes earlier, and then he ducked back behind a fried dough stand for cover.

"How long before Tyrell gets here with his team?"

"I contacted him at the same time I pinged you at the diner, but he and his men will arrive on the other side of the food court. I'm running this lift tube capsule as slowly as I can without being obvious, but if I confine our unwanted guest, he's armed well enough to cause some damage. I've dispatched a pair of my security bots directly through the closest access shaft and they'll be in position to protect Julie within seconds."

"Good job," Woojin said. "Since the assassin is only human, my stunner should put him down without a problem if I can just get in range."

"I have a better idea," the ship's AI told him as the lift tube capsule arrived.

A hard-looking man emerged, his head swiveling in all directions as if it was on a pivot. He strode aggressively to the food stall where Lume was still tidying up and addressed the Dollnick. Woojin couldn't hear the conversation, but he could see the alien pointing in the general direction of the diner with one of his upper arms. The assassin turned towards the captain's hiding place, took a few faltering steps, and then fell face forward without even putting out his hands to break the fall.

Tyrell and his security team reached the body at the same time as Woojin. A large kitchen knife protruded from the assassin's back.

"Missed his heart," the Dollnick cook commented. "I'm embarrassed he made it three steps, very sloppy. I'll have to get the Farling doctor to give me a human anatomy lesson. Hey, can somebody pass my knife back?"

"Captain?" the security chief asked.

"Looks dead to me," Woojin said, checking for a pulse on the man's neck. "Yup." He pulled out the knife and wiped it on the assassin's shirt before taking a few steps to return it to the Dollnick. "You are going to sterilize that, I hope."

"Silverware goes through the machine twice," Lume replied cheerfully. "It's one of Flower's rules."

"What do we do with the body?" Tyrell asked.

As if on cue, a pair of floating bots arrived and came into brief contact with each other, then slowly separated, extruding a transparent film between them until it was slightly longer than the corpse. Then they floated down near the deck, and Flower's voice spoke from one of their speaker grilles, "A little help?"

Tyrell nodded to his men and they lifted the corpse onto the improvised stretcher. As soon as their hands were out of the way, both bots effected a spin, sealing the body in film. Then they sped off with it to parts unknown.

"What about the blood?" Tyrell asked nobody in particular.

"I'll take care of it," Lume offered, coming out of his food stand with an mop and a bucket. "Flower just canceled my rent for the whole circuit."

"I owe you too," the captain said, offering his hand to the alien.

"I know," the Dollnick replied. "When will we be arriving at the next stop? I don't want to start prepping too early or the vegetables will spoil."

Eleven

"Do you still work for EarthCent?" the Galactic Free Press correspondent asked Woojin's wife. "The paper provided me with biographies of the senior officers but it wasn't clear on that point."

"Once a cultural attaché, always a cultural attaché, but as a reporter, you probably know what that means," Lynx replied.

"I mainly wrote about entertainment before I got married and joined my husband on board but I'm guessing you were the intelligence contact for the embassy."

"Yup. How long have you been with the paper?"

"Three years. It's funny that everybody calls it a paper when it's never been printed but it has a nice ring to it. Thanks for offering to introduce me to the old people who got scammed. It's an opportunity for me to do an investigative piece."

"They aren't that old," Lynx told her. "I mean, they're not young, but some of them are just recently retired."

"I guess they'll help offset all of the kids attending the boarding schools. I heard we picked up nearly five hundred new students at Break Rock," Dianne said.

"The number probably would have been higher if we hadn't brought them a new police force. I took a few groups of parents on tours and I could see how impressed they were with our facilities."

"You can't blame them. I was on Break Rock every day we were there to work on a story about the claim jumpers and your new police deployment. There's nothing for kids to do other than study with teacher bots or chase each other around the corridors. My editor pinged me this morning to say that they're dispatching a correspondent to do a follow-up in a few weeks."

"We won't be back this way for another six months so I guess your editor didn't want to wait for you to do it," Lynx said. "Do you mind if we stop by the nursery school on the way so I can check on my daughter? It's her first time."

"Oh no! Do you mean you put your daughter in nursery school in order to meet with me?"

"My husband and I have been planning it for months, though if we were back on Union Station, I would have stuck with InstaSitter and playgroups until Em was ready to start school. I sort of took it easy for a while after she was born, but I volunteered for Flower's third officer gig because I worry that my husband is stretching himself too thin. He's not a young man."

"I met Captain Pyun at one of my husband's business things," Dianne said. "He can't be much older than forty."

Lynx shook her head and made a small pointing up gesture.

"Forty-five? Come on, he can't be fifty."

"He recently turned sixty."

"Wow. He totally robbed the cradle."

"Thank you," Lynx said. She waved open the door of the lift tube capsule and the two women entered. "Em's nursery school, please."

"You could have just left her at home with me," the ship's AI complained. "I would have tasked a bot to play with her."

"It's not the same thing, Flower. She needs to be around other children, especially with a couple of late-in-life parents like Wooj and myself."

"You should have just started her in first grade then. She's smarter than all of the other children in the nursery school and she's just going to be bored."

"That's because you talk to her all the time."

"And thanks to me, she understands over two hundred words in Dollnick."

"I'm sure that will come in handy when she's old enough to whistle."

The capsule halted and Lynx led the way to the Little Pumpkins nursery school, which was located on the same deck as most of the boarding schools. A young woman who had registered Em that morning stopped the third officer at the door and asked, "Are you here to pick your daughter up early?"

"I just thought I'd check in and see how she was doing," Lynx said, craning her head around the nursery school teacher. "Hi, Em. Mommy is here."

"Could I speak to you in the corridor for a moment?" the woman asked with a tight smile.

"Uh, sure. Is something wrong?" Lynx asked.

"The captain was here two hours ago."

"He's a big softy. I swear he went into the bathroom to cry after he said goodbye to Em this morning."

"And he was here again one hour ago," the woman continued.

"Oh. That is a bit much, isn't it," Lynx said with an apologetic grimace. "I'll talk to him."

"And now *you're* here," the woman concluded, making it clear she wasn't at all happy. "I could understand the captain coming once to see his daughter and then returning because I didn't read him the riot act the first time, but I explained all of the rules to you when you registered Em. You know that having parents coming and going all day is confusing for the children."

"Is it? I guess I forgot. I'm so used to having Em with me most of the time."

"And you'll see her again when you come to pick her up, assuming the captain doesn't beat you to it. But until then, I'd appreciate if you'd follow the rules that you agreed to."

A chastised Lynx led Dianne back to the lift tube and instructed the capsule to take them to the independent living cooperative.

"Told you so," Flower said. "If I was babysitting Em, you could come and see her whenever you wanted."

The Galactic Free Press reporter shot Lynx a sympathetic smile, but they didn't speak again until arriving on the deck with the block of independent living cabins.

"What's the gravity here?" Dianne asked after her second step.

"Around eighty percent of Earth normal. It reduces strain on the heart for older people with circulatory problems, and it also lowers the risk of broken bones in case of an accidental fall." The third officer laughed. "I'm starting to sound like the advertising brochure they're working up."

"Advertising brochure?"

"I don't want to steal their thunder so I'll let them explain it to you."

"Thank you for coming," Jack greeted the two women when they arrived at the common room. "I got drafted to act as the temporary president of our committee because I stood up at the wrong time. Brenda here is an attorney and she can fill you in on the situation better than I could."

"This is Dianne, of the Galactic Free Press," Lynx introduced her companion, who displayed her press credentials on a lanyard hung around her neck.

"I've prepared a briefing document," Brenda said, handing each of the new arrivals a sheet of thick parchment. "I hope my printing is legible."

"It's better than some of those on-demand books my husband produces." Dianne held the sheet up close in front of her face and squinted. "Is this calligraphy?"

"My hobby is creating replicas of historical documents, mainly as gifts for friends, but I'll do anything to stay in practice. Why don't you each take a minute to run through the list and then Jack and I can answer any questions you have. I know you're familiar with most of this already, Lynx, but the committee has been hard at work since our last meeting."

"Can I get anybody a coffee?" Jack offered, after watching Dianne reach the end of the briefing sheet and turn it over to make sure there was nothing on the back. "Flower has a bot come around with a fresh urn every two hours between meals. It makes me wonder what they do with the old coffee."

"It goes right into the reservoir," the ship's AI informed them through the overhead speaker. "A little caffeine never hurt the fish."

"I should mention that as an officer, Flower has permission to listen in over my implant while I'm on duty," Lynx informed the others. "She could probably hear us anyway since the room is quiet, but I wanted you to know that whispering in my ear is no guaranty of confidentiality."

"Understood," Dianne said. "And thank you, Jack, but I had a coffee right before I came. This is a fascinating document and it would be wasted as a single story, even as a Sunday feature. The only problem I see from the standpoint of investigative journalism is that I have no way of getting the other side of the story. Even if the paper has a correspondent investigate on Earth, I doubt that the people who ripped you off are waiting around to give interviews."

"Do you think the paper would go for an extended series of articles?" Brenda asked eagerly.

"The Galactic Free Press is all about ongoing coverage. Staying with our stories is one of the things that sets us apart from all of the holographic news outlets that are focused on the latest disaster. I was telling Lynx on the way here that the paper will be sending a correspondent to follow up the article about claim jumping and the new police deployment I filed from Break Rock. I'm also going to do some pieces about the kids from there who signed up for our boarding schools."

"I wish all of the members of our new cooperative were willing to share their stories, but some of them are too embarrassed about getting conned," Jack said. "I've gone around and talked to everybody and you can count on twenty of us to answer any questions you have on the record. I don't know if your readers will be interested in a bunch of old fogies, but some of our members have led pretty interesting lives."

"Jack spent forty-five years working for the Dollnicks on their ag worlds," Brenda put in.

"I thought they offered excellent benefits," Dianne said.

"They do, but I took a cash buyout at the end of my first contract and blew it on the fantasy of becoming an independent trader," Jack said. "I wised up the second time around and took the pension option so I'll never have a problem paying my monthly bills, but I lost pretty much all of my savings on the Shady Oaks deposit."

"We have a mix of professionals and people who ran their own businesses, but Jack and the prospector who just joined us at Break Rock are the only ones who lived away from Earth all of their adult lives," the lawyer continued. "We're hoping to get a mix of people going forward, rather than turning into a community of expatriate retirees from Earth."

"Do you mind if I take some notes?" Dianne asked, removing her standard issue Galactic Free Press tab from her purse and instructing, "Record," before laying it on the table. "Independent living on Flower, rough notes. The way I see it, the first article should be a regular wide spectrum story about the fraud."

"Wide spectrum?" Jack asked.

"Do you guys subscribe to the paper?"

"I take the news and the legal sections," Brenda said.

"Agriculture and sports," Jack admitted sheepishly. "I kind of watch the Grenouthian channel for news, though I would check the free edition of the paper if there was a big story."

"And that's how it's supposed to work," Dianne told them. "Anybody can read the full edition with ads without a subscription, but we have section editors to curate the news for subscribers who sign up for specific interests. The paper ran an experiment once with sending an ad-free version of the whole paper to all subscribers, but it turned out that people were actually willing to pay more to read less."

"Back on Union Station we always got the full edition and it's too much to go through," Lynx interjected. "Woojin used to spend all Sunday morning glued to his tab trying to keep up with everything that was going on in the galaxy. The first thing I did when we took this job was to change our subscription to the new section edited specifically for Conference of Sovereign Human Communities members."

"Right. So what I'm getting at is that for maximum exposure, I'll have to write the first story in different versions. I think we might get the front page on a slow day with the basic fraud, but we'll also want to do a version specifically for retirees that would work in the Sunday 'Living' section, and another one focused on the numbers for the business section. I'm not a crime reporter, but maybe my editor can get one of our correspondents on Earth to write that version."

"We're really hoping that the paper's readers will be interested in the story of what happens next," Brenda said.

"You want free publicity," Dianne interpreted. "That's nothing to be ashamed of, everybody wants free publicity. You'd be surprised how much of our reporting on engineering projects comes to us in the form of press releases."

"Really?" Lynx asked. "I've never seen what I'd call a puff piece in the paper."

"Press releases are always fact-checked and rewritten by one of our tech correspondents. We live in a big galaxy and there's always something new being built, not even the engineering journals can report it all. The news of the year on some planet or giant space habitat is going to go unnoticed by the rest of the galaxy unless there's a clever promoter behind it."

"Or if it fails," Jack put in. "You can always count on the Grenouthians to broadcast a story about a runaway space elevator car, a major decompression accident, or a collapsed bridge."

"If you don't have death and destruction going for you, you have to persuade an editor that your story is worth reporting, though in this case, you have me to do that for you. Listen, do any of you have any journalism experience?"

"I wrote for the university law review, but I wouldn't call it journalism," Brenda said.

"Who, what, when, where, why," Dianne reeled off. "It's built into the story template on my tab. 'Who' is all of you as individuals, and also, your cooperative as a whole. 'What' is independent living, both the deal you originally signed up for and what you make out of it now. 'When' goes back to when you first met a Shady salesperson and extends into the future. 'Where' begins on Earth and ends here on Flower. And 'why' begins in greed and ends in altruism. We have the five elements of a great series of articles here, but it all starts with a news story about the scam."

"How much leeway does the Galactic Free Press give you in researching and reporting your own stories?" Jack asked.

"I'm on retainer to write two entertainment articles a month, plus reviews of any live performances I can get to, but that's basically a part-time job. I gave up working full time when I signed onto this ship, though I'm hoping to convince the paper that Flower deserves a full time correspondent. The problem is that you're too good at your jobs," she added, giving the third officer a dirty look.

"Excuse me?"

"When Flower first launched, the paper sent a correspondent out with you, and she landed a front page story at least once a week."

"Penelope," Lynx acknowledged. "She left halfway through our second circuit when things calmed down."

"Exactly. The first time you helped humans on an open world set up their own library with books from Earth, it was front page news. The second time it made the entertainment section. The third time it only mattered to the people who got the books."

"But Break Rock wasn't our first police deployment, or even the tenth, and you reported on that."

"Violence is different. If there weren't any problems on Break Rock and you brought them a police force with alien patrol craft, it might have gotten a mention in the shipping news, but not as a featured article. What I'm trying to get at is that your story will only work as a series if there are obstacles to overcome."

"Don't worry about that," Jack said. "A bunch of senior citizens with short-term memory loss trying to start their own independent living cooperative faces nothing but obstacles."

"In a way that's true, but there's a serious problem, at least from the standpoint of suspense."

"What's that?"

"Flower."

"I'm right here," the AI replied immediately.

"That's the problem," Dianne said. "I have a question for you, Flower. Say five thousand elderly people decided to sign up at the next stop. What would you do?"

"I'd activate enough bots to clean out more cabins on this corridor and add another fifteen thousand meals a day to the schedule."

"Where's the drama in that? If I was writing a story about your group opening an independent living facility on Earth, every new member would represent a challenge to house and feed. But Flower could probably gear up to handle a million new occupants overnight."

"Logistically, it would be difficult to board that many people in so short a time without a conveyer belt," the AI commented.

"So you're saying we need to exclude Flower from the process to make it harder than it could be?" Jack asked. He made a face. "I don't think that would be fair to our new members."

"And it wouldn't be ethical for me to report about artificial obstacles as if they were real," Dianne said. "I'm just saying that to get a series of articles out of this, we're going to need personal stories that go beyond simple facts and figures. You'll be able to get your point across that you're open for business, but nobody wants to read about Dollnick maintenance bots cleaning cabins."

"I do," the ship's AI retorted.

"I'll get to work on the basic story, and if you can arrange for me to meet the people willing to talk about their financial losses on the record, I can come back whenever it's convenient for them. If you lay out your plans with a time line, I'll look for a story hook I can use at each stage, and then we can coordinate as much as possible."

"Works for me," Flower said.

Twelve

"Wakey, wakey. Sheezle bugs and gravy."

"What?" Bill asked groggily. He'd been dreaming about picking an alien analog to cherry tomatoes on an ag world covered with endless vines of the fruit when somebody had turned on a radio that started playing a commercial jingle about bugs in an endless loop. "Radio. Turn off."

"I'm not a radio, though I am available to perform the wake-up call of your choice for a small recurring fee," Flower informed him. "The security chief is on his way to see you and you don't want to be in bed when he gets here."

"Alright, already. I'm—where are my clothes?"

"I had a maintenance bot undress you and send your clothes to recycling. Don't worry," the AI spoke over Bill's protests, "I had the bot go through your pockets first. I left you thirty creds for spending money and opened a ship's account for you with the programmable cred, which had one-hundred and two creds on it."

"I had a programmable cred?"

"You didn't know? That seems odd, even for a human."

Bill hesitated, and then realized he was about to repeat the story of his theft for the security chief anyway. "I took it from a gang member who was teaching me to work a stunner so I could mug miners."

"Good for you," Flower congratulated him. "Normally, programmable creds are keyed to the individual and won't transfer balances without voice confirmation, but as an authorized register dealer for the Stryx, I can override the lock-out for sums below ten thousand creds."

"I'm worth a hundred and thirty-two creds? I've never had that much cash in my life."

"Actually, you're worth a hundred and twenty-seven creds. I had a shop deliver a new set of clothes and charged it to your account. The proprietor discouraged me from ordering new shoes based on measurements, and your old boots were actually salvageable, though they'll be uncomfortably warm here."

Bill spotted the new clothes, underwear and all, neatly folded on the cabin's built-in desk, and he rolled out of bed to get dressed. He ended up on the floor.

"Do you require assistance?" Flower inquired.

"Muscle spasms." He tried rubbing his lower back and his abdomen at the same time, then grunted and forced himself to his feet. He didn't even bother trying to stand on one leg to get into the underwear, instead sitting on the chair and dressing himself with deliberation.

"I didn't know whether to get you boxers or briefs so I chose the boxer-briefs."

"I wondered what they were," Bill said, and winced as he bent to pull on the socks.

"Your guest is here," the Dollnick AI announced. The door to the cabin slid open, admitting a large man wearing the black fatigues favored by human mercenaries. "I'll let you two chat, but I expect him out in the corridor doing calisthenics in five minutes, Tyrell."

"Your wish is my command, Flower," the security chief responded. "Here," he added, offering a small box to Bill.

"It's a basic ear-cuff translator, compliments of the captain. When you earn some money you can rent or buy a better one."

"Thank you, sir."

"No need to 'sir' me, son. The captain informed me that you were stuck on an unlicensed picking crew before you won free and made your way to Break Rock where you were forcibly recruited by a gang. Sound familiar?"

"It's true," Bill insisted.

"What made you gamble on leaving Earth with a crooked contractor to start with? I ask because we're trying to crack down on them."

"My mom was in a Sun Cult, you know, where they give everybody crappy jobs selling stuff from pushcarts? She got me a free teacher bot, but we were busy all the time working and I was never that interested in studying. Then she married a creep from the cult who I couldn't stand so I went out on my own. I wanted to get off-world, but I failed a couple of tests for alien contractors. Then some guy who ran away from the cult a few years before me came back to the neighborhood. He spent money all over the place and told us he'd earned it on a traveling ag picker crew. The guy charged twenty creds a head to hook us up, and it turned out that the job was no better than being a slave!"

"Don't feel bad, it's been going on since ancient Egypt," Tyrell said. "Boy returns to his village after a long absence flashing a gold bracelet and saying he earned it picking corn in the Nile Delta. All the other hungry boys sign up, and it's not long before they find out the gold bracelet comes from selling slaves, not picking corn. I'll get the names and dates from you later so it can go into a database where smarter people than us might tie it all together. How about what happened on Break Rock?"

"I was starving and nobody would give me a job. Some guys spotted me going through the garbage and offered to share a meal, and after they fed me, they said I had to join their gang. I didn't want to do it, but they went ahead and initiated me anyway, six guys pounding on me with their fists and feet. I didn't have any choice but to go along with it after that, but when the guy assigned to teach me to rob people showed me how to use a stunner, I put him down with the first shot, took his money, and bought a shuttle ride to your ship."

"Smart kid," Tyrell said. "Those cheap stunners are only good for one shot per charge and he was probably counting on your at least testing it before trying it on him."

"Time," Flower reminded them.

"Alright, Bill. I wanted to double-check that the captain wasn't falling for a sob story but you ring true to me. We just dropped a police detachment at Break Rock and they'll clean out the gangs in no time, but stop by my office later and I'll have you look through some images to see if you can spot anybody involved in the illegal picking crew. Enjoy your calisthenics."

"Thank you. And thank the captain for this," he added, holding up the box with the translation device. After Tyrell exited, Bill struggled into his boots and then shuffled out of his cabin and leaned against the wall. A minute later, doors up and down the corridor slid open, and people, most of them in their late teens or early twenties, stepped out. The waitress from the diner emerged from the door directly across from his own, and a moment later, Flower's voice issued from every speaker grille with warm-up instructions.

"Morning," Bill grunted as he stretched to touch his toes, falling well short.

"Morning to you," Julie replied, her own hands flat on the deck.

"And reach," the AI's voice echoed through the residential deck. All up and down the corridor, the young people straightened up and stretched above their heads.

Bill heard a series of cracks coming from his vertebrae as he reached for the ceiling high over his head, and the bruises all over his body from the gang initiation started to ache again.

"What are you doing for a sport?" he asked Julie.

"Me? Theatre. Everybody tells me that I'm lucky I didn't join the ship a few years ago because they had like a thousand softball teams and it was just a big mess."

"Toes," Flower instructed, and everyone reached for the deck again. "I had sufficient space prepared on the ag decks to host a thousand games all at the same time if that's what was necessary," the AI continued in a low voice over a single speaker located above the two young people. "It's not my fault that everybody was so out of shape."

"I never even heard of softball before Dewey told me about it," Julie said. "Anyway, I do enough running around shelving books and waitressing that I think I should get a waiver."

"And reach. I don't count workplace activity as a team sport."

"I thought you said we have to play a sport to stay in shape," Bill objected.

"And to build team spirit and foster cooperation," the AI replied over the single speaker, before broadcasting, "Toes."

"I know I'm going to regret this, but do you have a sport recommendation for me?" Bill asked.

"Theatre. Lunge left."

"Is that a Dollnick sport?"

"That depends on the director," Flower replied. "Lunge right." Bill let out a yelp as a deep bruise on his thigh protested. "You can learn how to fight with muscle-powered weapons," the AI continued.

"Stage fighting?"

"Would you prefer if it were real fighting? Down and count."

"I don't know," Bill said, straightening back up after a ten count. "I don't think I could act in front of people."

"Twist left. Trust me."

"That's what you said about doing calisthenics and I think I'm dying."

"Don't exaggerate. Twist right and I'm registering you for theatre," the AI said. "Why aren't you twisting, Bill?"

"I can't move," the young man hissed between clenched teeth and took a tentative step forward. His hand reached for his lower back of its own accord.

"I hope that now you both see why daily stretching is so important. None of the others are suffering from muscle spasms." The ship's AI produced an exaggerated sigh. "Could you escort Bill to the med bay, Julie? It's on the library deck before the printer's."

"Does this mean I'm done stretching for the day?" she asked hopefully.

"I'll coach you through what you missed before bed."

Julie took two steps across the wide corridor and gave her full attention to her neighbor. "Wow, you really do look like you're hurting."

"It's not that bad," the young man said, taking a shuffling step with his hand glued to his lower back. "Funny that Flower gave me the cabin across from yours. You're the only person I know on board, other than the captain and the head of security who I just met."

"I was probably the last person to come aboard at Earth and you were probably the first to join after we left," Julie said. "I think she's just filling the cabins in order. The rest of this corridor is empty, which is why we're last in the stretching line."

"I don't have time for this," Bill groaned, trying to pick up his pace. "I've got to see the security chief at his office and look for work. Are you making a living at the diner? It didn't look very busy."

"It's just a part-time job for me. I actually work at the library as an intern twenty hours a week and that covers my room and board."

"How far is it to the lift tube? I wasn't really paying attention when Flower guided me home last night."

"There are lift tubes in every spoke ring, and fortunately, the on-demand book printer is inboard from the library, so we only have to make the next cross corridor. Flower could probably send a bot or something if you can't walk."

"No, it's not that bad. I guess cramming myself in under the merry-go-round didn't do me much good. I'm kind of a stowaway."

"That's cool," the girl said, raising her estimation of the skinny guy who looked like he'd spent too much time in the sun. "Here we are." They entered the lift tube capsule, which set off before the girl could give instructions.

"Library deck," Flower announced as the door slid open. "I've instructed the Farling to charge his repairs to the crew's account, so don't offer to pay."

"Repairs?" Bill asked as he shuffled out of the lift tube.

"I've never been to a doctor so I don't know how it works," the girl admitted. "I think that Farlings are some kind of aliens, though. It must be right here." She reached to knock on the doors adorned with an artistic representation of a skeleton, but they slid apart before her knuckles made contact. A man emerged from the med bay walking with a slight limp.

"And there's nothing wrong with your leg, it's all in your head," an angry voice called after him.

The patient gave the young people an embarrassed look and said, "I've had a bad hip for years and I guess the limp is just a habit."

"He couldn't help you?" Julie asked. "I thought alien doctors could fix anything."

"Oh, my boss brought me in because I crushed my hand in a chain hoist around twenty minutes ago," he said, holding it up for their inspection and flexing the fingers. "It looked like hamburger before Doc got started on it."

"You're lucky there weren't any broken bones."

"There weren't any intact bones left at all, just big chunks," the man told them, sounding almost proud of how badly his hand had been mangled. "Doc yelled at me the whole time he was fixing it up, but I was too zonked on the anesthetic to really understand him. Then he gave me a shot to clear my head and now my hand's all better, though it stings a little. Well, I better get back to work and clean up the bloody mess before it dries hard."

"Don't just stand there letting the cold air in," the alien doctor admonished the newcomers through the open doors. Both of the young people gaped at the giant beetle and remained glued to their spots. "Suit yourselves," the Farling told them, and the doors slid shut again.

"Why didn't you go in?" Flower demanded over a nearby speaker.

"He's an insect!" Julie protested.

"Don't be such a baby. Get in there and have Bill fixed so you can go to work."

If Julie hadn't been there, Bill probably would have shuffled away, but he didn't want to look weak in front of the girl, so he extended his arm and moved forward after the doors slid open.

"Congratulations, you passed the first test," the Farling said, glancing at a hologram of the young man's insides that materialized as the patient passed through the scanners at the entrance.

"What's that?" Bill asked.

"You're alive. I don't fix robots or artificial people. Now you."

"There's nothing wrong with me," Julie said. "I'm just on my way to work."

"I'm running a two-for-one special today, and if you're a good girl, you'll get a lollipop. Just walk through the door and then you can leave."

Julie entered the medbay against her better judgment and the doors slid shut behind her.

"Boy," the doctor said, turning his attention back to Bill. "You're covered with contusions and you have a fractured rib. Normally I'd tell you to let everything heal on its own, but since somebody else is paying, I think I can help things along. Raise your arms above your head."

Bill did as he was instructed, though he froze a few times as muscle spasms hit. The beetle stepped forward and whisked off the young man's T-shirt in one smooth motion. Julie gasped at the large yellow and black bruises left from the impact of many fists and boots from the gang initiation three days earlier.

"Now drop your pants."

"I'm not dropping—give me my shirt back!"

"Turn around," the doctor instructed, and when Bill failed to comply, grabbed the young man by the shoulders and turned him to face a chart on the wall. "What's the smallest line you can read?"

"What? It's not English."

"Try harder."

Julie found herself frozen in disbelief as the beetle took advantage of Bill's distraction to plunge a giant hypodermic needle into the patient's back and push in the plunger.

"A little bone cement," the doctor informed her conversationally as he pulled the needle back out, all of which passed without any reaction from Bill. "My own recipe." He swapped the hypodermic for what looked like a giant oven mitt and instructed the patient, "Now read the next line."

"It's still not English. Hey, that tickles."

Everywhere that the beetle rubbed the mitt on the young man's torso, the bruises were erased and the skin returned to its normal color. In less than a minute, the doctor finished his task and dropped the now-discolored mitt into a waste bin.

"If you won't remove your pants the contusions on your legs will have to take care of themselves."

"They're fine, really," Bill said, lowering his arms and looking down at his body. Then he raised his arms again and twisted from side to side when he realized the muscle spasms were gone. "How'd you do that?"

"You aren't equipped to understand. If you'll put on your shirt and wait outside, I need to speak with the young lady."

Bill looked over at Julie, who nodded, and then grabbed his T-shirt and slipped past her out the door.

"If you're going to give me instructions for taking care of him or something, we're just neighbors," Julie said.

"Try not to get upset by what the doctor is about to tell you." The note of concern that Flower injected into her artificial voice made a chill run down the girl's spine, and she turned to the giant beetle with questioning eyes.

"Your body is swarming with nanobots," the Farling informed her. "They're slowly assembling into a self-destruct device that you won't survive. The med bay scanners aren't designed to decipher nanotech coding, but I believe the swarm you are hosting represent a failsafe device that only activates after the prolonged absence of an external disarm signal. A few weeks away from the master transmitter, perhaps, and the absence of the suppression code triggers an unfortunate sequence of events."

"I thought your former associates on Earth might have tried something like this," Flower said. "Nanobots can be infiltrated into the body various ways, including through food and drink. You did say they had alien partners."

Julie felt strangely numb as she let the Farling guide her to the operating table, where he helped her up and then stretched her out on her back.

"Can you get them out?" she asked the doctor in a hollow voice.

"Yes. The nanobots in question are relatively low-tech but they are designed to terminate the host in a spectacular fashion. If the people who did this to you had gone for something less flashy, you'd be dead already."

"Flower?"

"Trust the doctor, Julie. I'll tell Bill that you have a lady issue and not to wait."

"Don't do that," the girl protested weakly, but her voice sounded far away, and the lights were growing dim.

"Try not to fight the anesthetic," the Farling instructed her. "I've already blocked the nanobots from accessing your brain, and if all else fails, I'll clone you a new body, move the spongy stuff over, and have you back on your feet in no time."

The last thing the girl heard was Flower's voice saying, "You may as well give her an implant while you have her open, M793qK. Put it on EarthCent's tab."

Thirteen

"I thought I'd be baking bread for humans," Harry complained after he finished jotting down Flower's verbal instructions for making what she called a Holiday Loaf.

"Where's the excitement in that?" the AI retorted. "Besides, this is a special day on our calendar so you'll be making several of my regulars very happy. Dollnicks believe that food for festive occasions should never be prepared by AI-controlled robots. The truth is they barely tolerate me cooking for them on regular days."

"But the cafeteria food you've been supplying to our independent living cooperative is terrific!"

"I know that, thank you, but Dollnicks, and most of the other advanced species for that matter, frown on the overuse of automation. They all place strict limits on the use of robotics, and food preparation is one of the areas where it's difficult to justify automation unless there simply aren't enough warm bodies available."

"I guess they've never visited an industrial bakery on Earth," Harry said, taking another look at his notes. "I think there's something wrong with these quantities. Are you sure you translated all of the alien measures into English correctly?"

"They aren't alien measures to me, and yes, math is actually one of my strong suits. What specifically bothers you?"

"Well, you've got twenty cups of flour and just a half an ounce of yeast. I would have figured at least double the amount, maybe triple."

"It's very aggressive yeast. It wouldn't be a bad idea to wear gloves."

"Really?"

"You don't want it getting on your skin or under your fingernails," Flower warned him. "You'll need seven cups of water and the yeast likes it hotter than your Earth varieties. In fact, just let the faucet run for a few seconds and I'll regulate the temperature."

Harry turned on the faucet, found a mixing bowl under the counter, and added seven measured cups of water. Then he self-consciously slipped on a pair of latex gloves before opening the package of yeast and dissolving it into the hot water.

"Wait thirty seconds before adding the tuber sugar and the salt. It lets the yeast work up an appetite."

"You're the boss," Harry said, referring to his instructions again. "No oil?"

"The egg is oily. You can whisk it while you're waiting to add the flour."

"Sure seems like a weird way to make bread. How can an egg be oily and why didn't the bot put it out for me?"

"Hard-shelled fish eggs are always oily, and being egg-shaped, they roll off the counter and make a mess," Flower replied. "A fresh carton was delivered just before you came in."

"Where is it?"

"In the egg cabinet. Where do human bakers keep eggs?"

"We use them up so fast that I just kept the cartons on the counter," Harry replied as he added the sugar and salt to the yeast mixture. It began to bubble vigorously. "Is it supposed to do that?"

"So far so good," the AI said. "I'll tell you when to add the flour. The egg cabinet is behind you to the left with the glass front."

"What are those big red things in it?"

"Eggs. Don't be surprised that the whites are black and the yoke is blue."

"I don't think anything would surprise me at this point," Harry muttered to himself, taking one of the large eggs from the cabinet. "It's not going to hatch on me, is it?"

"They aren't fertilized."

The baker found he needed both hands to crack the eggshell open on the edge of the sink and emptied the contents into a new bowl. The whisk had little serrations like saw teeth, but the resulting mixture had a distinct raw-egg-like texture, along with an oily film floating on the top.

"The egg is what makes it Holiday Loaf?"

"That and the quantity of tuber sugar. Over the last ten thousand years, some Dollnicks have started mixing in dried fruit, but I'm a purist. Go ahead and add the flour."

"An AI purist who's never eaten any of her own baking," Harry mused as he began mixing in the flour. "Does tradition mean I'll have to knead the dough by hand?"

"It's perfectly acceptable for a biological baker to use modern kitchen equipment," Flower replied. "The important thing is that you cook with the proper intent."

"And what's that?"

"You don't know? What did you study to become a baker?"

"Baking. What do Dollnicks study?"

"Metaphysics, though the schools call it culinary philosophy. You have to hold in mind that you're providing nourishment for your fellow sentients or the food loses half of its nutritional value."

"Do you actually believe that?"

The ship's AI lowered her voice. "Not really. You?"

"Bunch of alien bunkum if you ask me. Where's that kneading machine?"

"Next to the egg cabinet."

"The thing that looks like a dryer?"

"It also shapes and bakes the bread and is self-cleaning. Combine the ingredients now, set the dough in there between the paddles, and whistle the—I forgot you can't speak Dollnick. I'll turn the machine on, just don't tell anybody."

Harry placed the dough in the machine and latched the door. Then he reflexively looked around for the blackboard where Irene would list the baked goods she wanted for the storefront that day.

"Seems funny, coming in to work and baking just one loaf of bread. I can't remember the last time I mixed so little dough."

"By the time the yeast finishes doing its thing, the one loaf will be more than enough. I'll be surprised if half of it doesn't end up in the compost."

"How long will the whole process with the kneading, rising, and baking take?"

"Less than fifteen minutes," Flower replied. "The oven employs molecular—you wouldn't understand."

"Is this the kitchen where you have bots prepare the cafeteria food you've been sending us? I don't see any of the ingredients that we eat."

"I have hundreds of kitchens, though many of them are dedicated to baking. Remember that my standard complement on colonizing missions was five million, and while the families took care of most of the cooking at home, I employed nearly a thousand bakers. There's an old Dollnick saying that bread is the staff of life."

"I've heard that one," Harry said, without letting on where. "You have hundreds of kitchens this size?"

"Much larger. The kitchen you're in now is attached to the specialty cafeteria where I would serve alien observers who came along on colonizing voyages. Ironically, there are now so few Dollnicks on board that I can feed the half-dozen who are traveling without family in this cafeteria, along with the other single aliens."

"Is separating out the bachelors a cultural thing?"

"They take their meals in this cafeteria because they don't want to eat alone in their cabins. The Dollnicks running distribution businesses on Flower are traveling with their families, the same with the Grenouthian traders and most of the Drazen and Frunge bazaar merchants. But there are a few individuals from each species traveling alone for various reasons, so this cafeteria provides them a place to be together."

"I heard that all of the species keep to different length days. Are you open around the clock?"

"Yes, but those who don't want to eat by themselves have settled into an official schedule that mimics the main human shift. When in Fubreeze, do as the Fubreezians do."

"I've heard that one as well," Harry said. He was beginning to wonder if all the sentients in the galaxy shared similar sayings. "What will I be making for them to go with the bread?"

"There's leftover soup reheating on the stove. I had a bot put it on before you came in."

"How come I don't see any bots in here now?"

"I thought they might make you nervous. Humans are often uncomfortable working in close quarters with remotely controlled machines."

"You've got that right," Harry said. "It doesn't seem like much for a holiday breakfast, though. Bread and leftover soup. Isn't there something else I can make?"

"I'm afraid the main course this morning will be alcohol in its various forms."

"The aliens all drink?"

"Dollnicks limit their alcoholic intake to holidays and a narrow range of social occasions, but some members of certain other species are known to get sloppy at every opportunity," the AI informed him. "It's fortunate they insist on mixing their own drinks because I refuse to participate."

"But who drinks at breakfast?"

"Species who limit their alcohol intake to holidays and a narrow range of social occasions."

"Wait a second. If there are going to be non-Dollnicks here, what will they eat?"

"Both the Holiday Loaf and the soup are recipes which are digestible by all of the species who will be present, though the Frunge won't eat the bread for cultural reasons and the Drazens pour hot sauce on theirs. Over the course of hundreds of thousands of years, the oxygen-breathing species tend to develop a tolerance for a subset of each other's basic foodstuffs. Generally speaking, the older the species, the wider their range, though the Drazens are the exception to the rule."

"Which ones are they again?"

"Humanoids not unlike yourself, other than the tentacle and the extra opposing thumb," Flower replied. "They evolved what humans call 'cast iron stomachs' before they even joined the tunnel network, though it's not a very efficient system."

"Being able to eat everything isn't efficient?"

"What doesn't kill them, which is pretty much everything, doesn't necessarily make them stronger. They just pass it through without harm. Would you like to meet one? Jorb just came in and he's alone."

"I don't know, Flower. I appreciate your giving me this ear-cuff translator for work, but other than realizing that all that whistling in your lift tube capsules was actually singing, I haven't really tested it."

"Then meeting the diners will give you an opportunity to adjust. There's nothing left to do in here until they start asking for drinking snacks after the meal, and that's just a matter of putting some sliced vegetables on plates. There are already buckets of them prepared in the fridge."

"Why did you do all the prep work when you knew that I'd be here?"

"I was afraid you might back out," Flower said. "It wouldn't be the first time a human changed his mind at the last minute."

"Can't argue with you there," Harry said. "I've had a few new hires not show up for their first day of work when they realized that waking up at three in the morning wasn't as exciting as they thought it would be. Lead on, MacDuff."

"Through the swinging door with the blue light, and I believe you're misquoting Shakespeare."

"I know it's 'Lay on, MacDuff,' but language evolves over time. Where did you hear about Shakespeare?"

"I've read the full corpus of human literature available in electronic form, and the Grenouthian theatre director on board has produced a number of Shakespeare's works for team activities. Don't forget you have your first rehearsal this evening."

"You're starting to remind me of my wife," Harry grumbled, approaching the door that Flower had indicated led to the dining area. "What does the blue light mean?"

"That the safety is off because the swing area on the other side is clear. If the light is green, the safety is on and the door won't open."

"Why doesn't it slide like the rest of the doors on the ship?"

"Because it's automatic and you wouldn't want the waitstaff colliding with each other in full stride. The swinging door functions as a turnstile."

Sure enough, the door swung open as soon as Harry stepped into the sensor range, and he saw that the cafeteria was even smaller than the common room where the independent living cooperative took their catered meals. If Flower hadn't told him that the room's sole occupant was an alien, the baker might have taken him for a human.

"Welcome," the Drazen greeted Harry enthusiastically, jumping up from his seat and offering his hand. "Jorb is the name, I just came aboard at Union Station a few weeks ago. I'm starting a dojo if you're interested in studying martial arts," he added. "My card."

Harry flinched as the Drazen enlisted a tentacle that grew out of his back from between the shoulder blades to present a plastic chit.

"I'm a bit old for martial arts so I'll let you save the card for a potential customer," Harry said. He ignored the plastic chit and shook the Drazen's hand, which felt a bit odd when the alien's extra thumb folded around the bottom of his wrist.

Jorb looked hurt and returned the chit to the breast pocket of his shirt. "I was just trying to be friendly," he muttered.

Something about the way the alien moved his lips led Harry to ask, "Were you speaking English just now?"

"Of course," the Drazen said, perking back up at the new opening. "I picked a little up from my Human friends on Union Station and I've been cramming it since joining Flower. You couldn't tell?"

"This is my first time wearing an ear-cuff translation device," Harry explained. "I didn't know if I was hearing it or you."

"Those external translators can't cancel out the source so you would have heard me speaking Drazen in your other ear if I wasn't talking English," Jorb explained. "Are you sure you won't take my card?"

"Sure, I'll have one," Harry said. He pulled out a chair across the narrow table from where the Drazen had been sitting. "Are you early for breakfast or are the others all late?"

"Can you keep a secret?" Jorb asked, handing over the plastic chit.

"As well as the next man," Harry replied. The Drazen frowned and remained silent, so the baker amended himself. "I mean, yes."

"I wanted to be here before any of the Dollnicks came in so I could claim to be in a hurry today and leave before they get too festive. I like a drink as well as the next Drazen, but I'm working at the finishing school in an hour and I have to be sharp for that."

"Finishing school?"

"I work part-time in a school for young ladies run by a Vergallian. The girls practice their self-defense on me,"

Jorb explained. "Ah, here comes Lume. He owns a salad bar in the food court."

A giant Dollnick strode up to the table and took the chair next to Harry, offering the human a handshake with one of his lower arms.

"Happy Nesting Day," Lume whistled.

"Happy Nesting Day," the Drazen responded, with Harry echoing him a fraction of a second later. "I hear you hit Flower's jackpot," Jorb added.

"Free rent for the rest of the circuit just for cleaning up a bit of criminal trash," the Dollnick boasted as he reached for the decanter at the center of the table and poured himself a glass of purple liquid. "Not joining me?"

"Just one," Jorb said, holding up the empty glass from his place setting for Lume to fill. "Don't offer any to Harry. You know Humans have weak stomachs."

"That's what keeps my salad bar in business," Lume concurred, offering Harry a companionable wink. "Did you two hear about what M793qK found in the body of a female who came on board at Earth?"

"Harry is a retired baker who I've talked into coming to work for me part-time," Flower interrupted. "He baked your Holiday Loaf."

"That's great," Lume said, though Harry thought that the alien's body language had suddenly become more guarded. "Not as a cover job? You were always a full-time baker?"

"Over forty years," Harry replied. "What do you mean by a cover job?"

"Many of us bachelors work two jobs while we're saving for marriage, and we call the second job the 'cover' because it's on top of the first," Jorb explained smoothly. "Was this your first time making Holiday Loaf?"

"I've prepared all sorts of special breads for human holidays, mainly religious festivals, but this is my first experience baking for aliens." He paused and looked at the Drazen and Dollnick in turn. "My wife always accuses me of being insensitive so maybe I should ask if it bothers you guys when I call you aliens."

"Not me," Lume said. "Everybody is an alien to somebody. It's as good a label as any as long as the context is clear."

"Yeah, but it can be confusing to figure out who you're referring to in mixed crowds," Jorb added. "Like, look at the alien who just walked in."

Harry followed the direction the Drazen was indicating with a hand held flat, both thumbs tucked in, and did a double-take when he saw a three-hundred pound bunny hopping into the room alongside a wiry-looking humanoid with vines in the place of hair.

"I see what you mean," he said. "Is the big one a Grenouthian? I'm starting theatre tonight as my required team sport and I heard that the director is one of them."

"You heard right and that's him," Lume replied. "You can just call him Director because they don't share their names outside of their species. The little fellow is Razood, and he's a blacksmith."

"A blacksmith? On a faster-than-light spaceship?"

Jorb leaned over the table and whispered to Harry behind his hand, "It's an affectation. The Frunge are all nuts about metal-working. Some aliens are like that."

"Who's the new ghost?" the giant bunny inquired.

"He's a baker working for Flower," Lume explained hastily. "Harry only has the one job. He baked our Holiday Loaf."

"And it's almost ready to come out of the oven," Flower announced.

"I better go check," Harry said, getting up from the table and heading back through the swinging door with the blue light into the kitchen. "Why did he call me a ghost, Flower?"

"It must be a new slang term for humans because you get so pale in space. Maybe I should turn up the ultraviolet in your living areas."

"Why would a giant white rabbit think that I'm pale?"

"Compared to the Drazen, you are pale. All of you furless two-armed humanoids do look awfully similar."

"He has a tentacle and extra thumbs!"

"Minor details," Flower replied as the door of the combination kneading machine and oven popped open.

"Is there an oven mitt or a wood paddle I can use to get the loaf out?" Harry asked.

"It's not hot," the Dollnick AI informed him. "I used the old thermal transfer trick to crash cool the loaf to serving temperature so it can be sliced. If I gave Lume an excuse to wait another hour, he'd drink himself under the table."

Fourteen

Tyrell walked Bill through the bazaar, introducing the young man to merchants and asking about job openings. A few of the traders were willing to give Bill a shot, but he balked at selling women's clothes, craft jewelry, and hand-woven carpets.

"I don't see myself sitting cross-legged on a blanket and bartering," Bill told the security chief apologetically. "It's not that I don't appreciate the offers, but Flower said I could always work on one of her ag decks, and at least I have experience as a picker."

"Don't you want to learn something new?"

"I don't know. I mean, sure, but I wasn't very good about keeping up with my teacher bot."

"Nobody on board is going to make you do anything you don't want to do, except maybe Flower, and she does that to everybody," Tyrell said. "How about working with your hands? We have a number of craftsman on board."

"Could I get into your police academy? I tried to join a mercenary unit back on Earth, but first they said I was too young, and then they said I wasn't in good enough shape."

"Carrying a weapon is a lousy way to make a living unless you luck into the honor guard for a royal on some alien world. You're welcome to join one of our self-defense classes, but we only take ten-year veterans from the mercenaries for the police training program."

"Why's that?"

"Most of them already have experience working police details for the aliens in multi-species settings, and to be perfectly honest, EarthCent would just as soon there weren't so many unemployed mercenaries wandering around. This way we get to kill two birds with one stone. How about blacksmithing?"

"Huh? You mean shoeing horses or something?"

"There's another name for that—farrier, I think. Razood is a nice guy and it wouldn't hurt you to get some experience with an alien."

"What kind?"

"Frunge. Razood is built wiry like you but their muscles are a lot stronger than ours. They look sort of human, except for the part about having evolved from their world's version of trees."

"Oh, yeah. The ones who bought up all the northern forests on Earth. Will he be able to understand me?" Bill asked, checking to see that his ear-cuff translator was in place.

"The adult aliens on board have implants that translate all of the tunnel network languages."

"So why do we even have a blacksmith on a spaceship?"

"Colonial Jeevesburg. It's one of our most popular tourist attractions after the bazaar and the amusement park. If you're still with us in six months when we stop back at Union Station, make sure to visit the medieval castle in Libbyland. Supposedly that's where the idea for Jeevesburg came from, but I've heard there are some reconstructed villages from the pre-industrial era back on Earth. Alien tourists go in big for that sort of thing."

The blankets piled with goods gave way to an area demarked by some sort of glowing energy field, and the security chief steered the young man around the barrier.

"Practice range," he told Bill. "All of the armorers have their booths to the side down there. The field set up by Flower will safely dissipate the discharge of any of the energy weapons for sale, not to mention absorbing the momentum of projectiles ranging from rail gun pellets to thrown knives."

"Anybody can buy weapons on board? Doesn't that lead to a lot of crime?"

"It's not quite as safe as living on a Stryx station, but Flower will drop a bot on anybody she sees misbehaving. Don't forget that we're actually living on a Dollnick colony ship that was built to go anywhere in the galaxy and support the terraforming and founding of a new world. Not long after I took this job, I asked Flower about coordinating with us on a plan to repel boarders and she brought me to her armory, or one of them. She's got enough military bots in storage to take over Earth if she had any interest in doing so and the Stryx didn't stop her."

"So who's actually running this ship?" Bill asked. "Is it the captain or is it Flower?"

"That depends which one of them you ask," Tyrell replied with a laugh. "The bottom line is that Flower and the ship are a single package, and she doesn't take orders from the captain as much as they discuss things and arrive at a mutually agreed upon course of action. If there isn't enough time to argue it out, Flower acts first and makes excuses later. This whole mission is basically a probationary job for her while she tries to rehabilitate herself in the eyes of the Dollnicks."

"What's she rehabilitating herself from?"

"She used to have," Tyrell paused and made air quotes around the next word, "issues with carrying out orders from her crew. They eventually abandoned ship, and I guess she had it pretty rough until the Stryx took her under their wing and set us up together."

"So we aren't the only Stryx welfare cases in the galaxy."

"I wouldn't call Flower a welfare case. More of a project. And here we are," the security chief concluded as they approached an improbable stockade fence and passed under a large sign that read "Colonial Jeevesburg." A smaller font below the name informed the visitors, "Sponsored by SBJ Fashions."

Bill couldn't help stopping repeatedly to stare at the various craftsmen working in open shop spaces. There was a cooper hand-finishing barrel staves, a shoemaker surrounded by wooden forms for different sized feet, a candle maker, a milliner, and even an apothecary shop, which was packed with people who were actually purchasing various herbal remedies. There were also several weavers, a tailor, and various food shops, including one selling smoked meats that were made on the premises. Up against the back wall of the stockade, between the silversmith and a pub, was the blacksmith shop.

"Greetings, Tyrell and friend," a rough-skinned alien with close-cropped vines on his head in the place of hair called in a voice like a creaky hinge.

"May the sun nourish your seedlings," the security chief replied politely. "You mentioned that you were looking for an apprentice and Bill here is interested in learning a trade."

The Frunge stepped forward, thumped on the young man's chest, squeezed Bill's biceps in an iron grip, and gave a noncommittal nod. Then he launched into a description of the duties of an apprentice in language that would have kept a team of lawyers busy for a week.

Bill listened to the translation through the loaner earpiece from the ship's stores, doing his best to ignore the noise from the alien's raspy speech. He began to understand why anybody who could afford it would buy an implant that canceled out the sound of the language being translated.

"It sounds really good, the parts I understood, but I kind of need to earn money to live on."

The Frunge exchanged a long look with the security chief and then shrugged. "I'll cover your room and board as long as it's less than two hundred creds a cycle, but I'll expect seventy hours a week out of you."

Bill's eyes narrowed and he clenched his jaw. The deal offered was barely better than the crooked labor contract he'd run out on, but the security chief was looking at him expectantly and he didn't want to appear ungrateful. "I don't know what room and board costs, but if two hundred creds a cycle will cover it, you've got an apprentice."

"You'll make your expenses with a little pocket change left over," Tyrell told the young man. As he turned to leave, he added over his shoulder, "By the way, those ear-cuff devices are notoriously bad at calendar terminology because they translate the units without doing the math. The Frunge day is roughly twice as long as ours and they have eight of them in a week. He's hiring you for a part-time job."

"A part-time apprenticeship," the alien corrected the departing security chief. "Is Bill really your name? Is it intended as a joke, like an overdue bill, or a bird's bill?"

"It's short for William, I think. My mother never said for sure. Tyrell told me your name but I'm not sure about the pronunciation."

"I'm Razood. Put on my spare leather apron there and we'll get started."

"Did you make all of these swords?" Bill asked, unable to hide his admiration of the impressive collection.

"I have a couple weeks to kill every time we park in Earth orbit taking on people and supplies for a new circuit," the alien replied modestly, starting Bill off on a new set of calculations to come up with the actual time it had taken. "Some of the swords date back to when I joined Flower for her first circuit because they aren't selling very well. I always thought your people spent most of their free time slaughtering each other so maybe my prices are too high. Hopefully, having a Human on the bellows will encourage others of your species to at least stop and look."

"I think we prefer slaughtering each other with guns," Bill said, though this admission made him feel oddly embarrassed. He looped the top strap of the heavy apron around his neck and tied it behind his back. "Do you get any alien customers?"

"Sales to members of the other species are what keep me in business. I sold a fine axe to a young Drazen yesterday, and a set of throwing knives to a Dollnick earlier in the week."

"You only make weapons?"

"I can make anything, but we measure a smith's skill by his edged weapons. I'm also a certified metallurgist and I consult for miners and prospectors. If you stick it out, I'll try to teach you how to assay minerals, though I'm told that your sense of taste is barely good enough to tell the difference between rock and metal."

"I think my earpiece may have glitched," the apprentice said. "You'll teach me to do what to minerals?"

"Assay. Determine the chemical composition. Miners need to know whether the ore they're digging up is going to pay for itself once it reaches the smelter. Here, you work the bellows while I heat up this rod stock. I got a special order from Flower for scrollwork brackets this morning."

Bill took hold of the long lever the alien indicated and began working it vigorously up and down.

"Don't try so hard," Razood cautioned him as the fuel in the forge began to glow white hot around the end of the long iron rod. "Slow and steady."

"Where's the smoke?"

"It's clean coke, and if you look up you'll see there's a fume hood with negative pressure above us. It's not very traditional, but one has to make compromises to work in space, and our sponsor pays the bills."

"For the fume hood?"

"My floor rent and a stipend as well. It wouldn't have made economic sense for me to open a smithy on a ship full of Humans otherwise. All right," Razood continued, pulling the glowing end of the long rod out of the fire. "You hold the dumb end so the heated section rests on the anvil and I'll start working the bend."

The apprentice followed the Frunge's order without causing any disasters, and the next hour flew by with alternating sessions of heating and bending until the fancy bracket was completed.

"I've never helped with anything like this before," Bill said, admiring the work. "What's the ship going to use it for?"

"It's a decorative mount for a security camera. The first order was for twenty units and Flower insinuated that if she likes the work there will be more to follow. She has excellent taste for an AI."

"I thought the Dollnicks were ahead of most species in engineering. Couldn't the ship have manufactured its own brackets?"

"They wouldn't have been authentic handmade scroll-work," Razood explained.

"That's another thing I don't get. Why doesn't the ship just do everything with bots? Why doesn't everybody do everything with bots? I worked on a picker crew that went from ag world to ag world on the tunnel network and every planet we visited had a space elevator! Why do species with space elevators need people to pick produce?"

"Thank you for reminding me that Humans have barely entered the machine age," Razood said, drawing another rod from his stock and indicating the bellows lever with a nod of his head. "It's a dangerous time for species when they find out they can replace labor with machines and brains with AI. The ones who get too caught up in it end up replacing themselves entirely, or they simply fade away as their populations dwindle. Look around the tunnel network and you'll see that all of the member civilizations put limits on using robotics to replace labor."

"But how about the AI, then?" Bill asked between heaves on the bellows. "Why wouldn't they keep multiply-ing on their own?"

"To what end? To use up all the local resources making more copies of themselves until all of the matter in the galaxy has been transformed into thinking machines? And what then? Anyway, the Stryx supposedly keep an eye on all of that so it doesn't get out of hand. Here, hold the rod for me."

Another hour passed in creating an elaborate scroll-work camera bracket and then the smith called break time.

"So what's the difference between aliens using bots to harvest their crops and hiring a bunch of humans to do it?" Bill asked, having had time to mull over the Frunge's lecture.

"That's just economics," Razood said. "When your people figure out a better way to make a living, the farmers will have to pay higher wages or find somebody else to do the work. The Dollnicks are the only tunnel network species that's really big on ag worlds, and that's mainly due to the fact that they like terraforming planets and need something to do with them. My own people prefer food from local farms."

"But farm labor pays next to nothing compared to good jobs."

"Farm workers are among the most respected and well-paid members of Frunge society. Few of my people have the fortitude to work shoveling manure all day long, which is why the wages are so high."

"The opposite is true on Earth."

"It's just a phase your people are going through," Razood said. "Every other species I know pays the highest wages for labor intensive jobs, especially those that involve working alone."

"Like blacksmithing?"

"That's the exception that proves the rule. Everybody wants to be a blacksmith." Razood picked up a watering can from the workbench and sprinkled the contents on his own head before continuing. "The only drawback is that the heat dries out my hair vines."

"In the neighborhood where I grew up, there was a sort of a labor exchange where you could stand around all morning waiting to get hired for a day's work. Even if you got a job, half the time the employer tried to cheat you on the pay."

"It's no wonder the Stryx had to open your planet early to save you from yourselves," the Frunge observed. "They rarely extend a tunnel network invitation to a species that hasn't developed interstellar travel. It's not surprising more than half of your people have abandoned their homeworld in less than a century."

"If I could have found work on Earth that would pay for a decent place to live I never would have left."

"I remember now," the alien said. "I saw a Grenouthian documentary about this. Your people already do try to use machines for everything, don't they? Did your leaders expect that all the idle hands would spend their time writing poetry and that somebody would pay to listen to it? Look, let me give you a bit of advice. I read a translated version of your Galactic Free Press to keep an eye on metal prices and I've noticed that your reporters always refer to the rest of us as advanced species. There's a reason for that."

"I thought it was your technology, faster-than-light drive and all that."

"All that?" The Frunge blacksmith began to laugh, a sound like sawing wood. "Do you imagine that every alien spends a hundred years in school learning the higher math that makes jump ships possible? Technology isn't who we are, it's just a tool, like my hammer," he added, striking the anvil for emphasis. "Look at the older tunnel network species like the Verlocks. Sure, they have magnetic monopoles and they even dabbled in their own cut-rate version of the tunnel network in the past, but you wouldn't know it talking to one of them."

"They opened a math academy in my neighborhood for smart kids but I was already too old for it. I'm sure I would have failed the entrance exam anyway."

"Well, the Verlocks do like their math, but they believe in magic too. All I'm saying is that technology is a means to an end, and if your goal is to make yourselves obsolete, you don't need faster-than-light drive to do it. Just replace your children with cute robots who actually do what they're told and in a generation you'll all be gone. Now grab another rod out of the pile. We have eighteen more camera brackets to make."

Fifteen

"Do I have permission to communicate with you directly over your new implant, Julie?"

"Sure, I guess," the girl replied to the ship's AI. "But isn't it going to look weird when I reply, like I'm talking to myself?"

"The Farling doctor also implanted a subvocalization pickup in your throat that will allow me to hear your spoken words if you aren't in range of one of my microphones," Flower explained. "With enough practice, most Humans can subvoc intelligibly without making any sound, though people who learn later in life may end up whispering."

"Did you say that out loud or in my head?" Julie whispered.

"In your head, and your lips are moving. Are you looking forward to your first theatre rehearsal?"

"Do you mean we're going to be staging a play?" the girl asked, her lips slightly parted like a ventriloquist feeding lines to a dummy. "I thought it would be more of a workshop."

"Don't focus on your mouth. It's all about breath control, or so I'm told. And the Grenouthian who runs our theatre believes that putting on a production is the only way to learn what's involved."

"I've never been very good at memorizing. I knew people on Earth who could do whole scenes from the immersive dramas they watched, but I have enough trouble remembering my new name. Hey, since you can speak directly in my head..."

"You want me to feed you lines? That would be cheating. Besides, if I agree to do so now it will only make it harder for you to learn the script on your own."

"So you aren't completely rejecting the idea."

"I don't know why I put up with you," Flower said in exasperation. "Most Humans find me intimidating."

"You probably feel sorry for me because you know that sooner or later I'm going to be killed by a syndicate assassin."

"Not on my ship, you aren't. I do wish you would stop being so morbid and agree to help with the library's reading program for children. It would cheer you up to spend some time around the little ones."

"Whether or not we talk about it I have a big fat target on my back," Julie said firmly. "I'm not going to be responsible for getting somebody's kid killed."

"Very well, it can wait, but I want you to take your self-defence training seriously while you're here. I can protect you while you're on board but I won't force you to remain."

"What self-defence training?"

"I meant theatre practice. You're going to be late if you don't get going."

Julie exited her cabin and impulsively knocked on the door across the corridor. The metal turned out to be thicker than she thought and it felt like she had rapped her knuckles on the door of a bank vault. She shook her head in disgust and was turning away to head for the lift tube when the door slid open.

"Hi," Bill said. "Flower told me you knocked. Ready to learn some acting?"

"No. You?"

"No. I asked Flower if I could change to something else but she said it's already too late and that I need to learn how to honor my commitments. Then she said a hundred other things until I got sick of listening to her and gave in."

"She's pretty persuasive," Julie allowed as they navigated their way to the lift tube together and entered the capsule. "Theatre, please."

"I missed you at calisthenics this morning," Bill said. "Are you feeling better after your, uh..." His question ground to a halt and his face colored.

"I'm fine, and it wasn't whatever Flower told you," Julie said. There was no way to explain to him about the nanobots that the beetle had found in her body without giving away her secret identity, though she was beginning to suspect that her presence on the ship was more widely known than was ideal for a witness protection program. "Flower said something that makes me think our theatre course might include some sort of self-defence training."

"That would be great. I'm tired of getting beat up wherever I go. And Razood says that if I want to stay on as his apprentice I have to learn enough about swordplay to fake it for the customers."

"Who?"

"Razood, the Frunge blacksmith who works in Colonial Jeevesburg," Bill said, as they exited the capsule on a deck neither of them had ever visited.

"To the left," Flower instructed.

"This way," Julie told Bill after realizing that the AI had spoken directly over her implant. "How did you find a job with a blacksmith?"

"After I left you at the doctor's, the ship's security officer took me around the bazaar and introduced me to some people. It's only part-time so I'm going to start working afternoons in one of Flower's cafeterias on her recommendation. I've picked enough crops to be curious to see what happens to them next."

"In here," Julie said, again responding to one of the AI's cues. "Wow!"

"Wow is right," Bill echoed her. They were standing at the top of an aisle that ran between what seemed like endless rows of Dollnick-sized seats reaching toward a tiny stage. "How many people do you imagine this theatre seats?"

"Five thousand," Flower responded over the public address system. "I have ten similarly sized venues on this deck."

"How could anybody seated this far back possibly hear? Is that the Grenouthian director on stage? He looks like a stuffed bunny I had when I was a child."

"Dollnick whistling carries much farther than primitive human speech and the acoustics in this room are perfect for the appropriate frequency range. Now get down there before you're late and the director makes you stay after class."

"Yes ma'am," Julie muttered, and joined Bill in hurrying down the sloping aisle. It still took nearly a minute to reach the stage, which didn't look nearly as small as it had from the back of the theatre. She looked suspiciously at the large bunny who was impatiently tapping a furry foot. "Are you the Grenouthian who offered me a bag of—"

"No," the director interrupted, the voice from his external translation device coming out like a shout. "Another thirty seconds and you would have been less than two minutes early. If you can't do better next time, don't come at all."

"We're early and you're yelling at us?"

"Not early enough. Now, do either of you have any martial arts training?"

"I have a pretty good idea where to kick a male," Julie replied irritably.

"Go ahead and try it," the director invited her.

"I'm not going to kick you."

"How about him?"

"I'm not going to kick Bill either."

"You didn't even look where I was pointing," the bunny barked at her, keeping his arm extended. Julie glanced in the direction indicated and saw another alien approaching at a run.

"Jorb," the Drazen introduced himself, panting slightly from his exertion. "Sorry I'm almost late. Flower only told me I was expected five minutes ago. What did I miss?"

"The young lady was about to kick you between the legs?"

"Why?" Jorb asked the girl.

"Ask the fur ball. It was his idea."

The director rolled his large black eyes towards the ceiling as if to ask what he had done to deserve such a fate. "Just because the male of a species has two legs you can't assume that his sensitive bits are dangling between them waiting for you to make contact with your foot. More importantly, Jorb and myself are trained martial artists, and attempting to kick either of us would leave you open to a counterstrike which exposes a fundamental flaw in your self-defence strategy."

"What does any of this have to do with theatre?" Julie demanded.

"I refuse to teach stage fighting to anybody who hasn't mastered the basics of self-defence first. It's in my contract."

"How about you?" Bill asked the Drazen. "Are you an actor?"

"I'm here because Flower requested I help train the two of you in martial arts. We'll be meeting every evening an hour before theatre team practice."

"Just like that?" Julie asked. "Flower snaps her fingers and every alien on the ship jumps to do her bidding?"

"Actually, she's letting me out of participating in a miserable human sport I signed up for by accident. I can spend all night running and none of them ever kick the ball in my direction even though I'm open. The other players don't even know the rules!"

"Not this again, Jorb," Flower's voice came over a nearby speaker.

"It's true," the Drazen protested. "I read the official rulebook myself and there's nothing in there about touching the ball with your tentacle. It's hand-balls that are forbidden."

"So you're going to teach us sword fighting?" Bill asked eagerly.

"That's the plan," Jorb said, casting a sour look in the direction of the speaker Flower had activated. "I brought these." He fished in a pouch and produced what looked like four small rolls of paper with protruding handles.

"Good," the bunny grunted, accepting one roll handle-first. He flicked his paw and a spiral of paper shot out to about the same length as his furry arm. He gave it an experimental swish or two in the air, and then shouted, "En garde."

The Drazen thrust two of the remaining rolls at Bill and then deployed his own paper sword while dancing out of the Grenouthian's reach. "Watch our footwork," he instructed the dumbfounded humans.

The two aliens launched into a furious series of thrusts and parries, their round paper swords making an odd ticking sound on contact. After nearly two minutes of acrobatic fighting, the bunny got past Jorb's guard and plunged the drawn-out spiral roll into the other alien's chest, causing the paper to rewind itself on the handle.

The Drazen staggered back and let his own paper roll fall before he declaimed, "The rest is silence," and collapsed to the stage.

The Grenouthian struck a pose and declared, "Now cracks a noble heart. Good night, sweet prince. And flights of angels sing thee to thy rest."

Bill began clapping loudly and Julie couldn't stop herself from joining in. The director helped the Drazen to his feet and both aliens took a bow.

"Was that from a Vergallian drama?" Bill whispered to the girl, still clapping.

"Shakespeare," she whispered back. "Hamlet. It was the most popular play on our teacher bots."

"Now," the director said. "Deploy your blades. All it takes is a flick of the wrist, and there's a stop to keep them from unraveling."

Julie accepted one of the paper rolls from Bill and followed the bunny's instructions, but it took her three attempts to get the spiral of paper fully extended.

"How can these things possibly hold up when we fight with them?" she asked.

"It's a combination of the spiral form and the special wax coating," Jorb informed her. "If you lock blades and push against each other with all of your weight, the paper spiral will deform easily enough, but as long as you're only using your wrist strength they'll hold up for dozens of dueling sessions."

"You take the boy and I'll take the girl," the director instructed. "Teach him the basic forms and we'll have them spar later—loser buys the drinks."

"I have to buy everybody drinks if I lose?" Bill asked.

"The bet is between Jorb and myself," the bunny said. "You couldn't swallow our version of adult beverages without doing irreparable harm to your digestive track."

The next forty-five minutes went by so quickly that Julie could hardly believe it when the other members of the theatre team began trickling in. Then the Grenouthian and the Drazen insisted that the pair of young humans square off against each other for a quick duel.

"Do we have to?" Bill asked. "I don't want to hurt her."

"With a paper spiral that weighs less than a coin?" Julie retorted dismissively. "I think you're just scared."

Bill's complexion turned darker, and he growled, "En garde." After the first few passes, both students forgot everything they had just learned and found themselves swinging at each other wildly.

"Eyes open!" the Grenouthian thundered at Julie.

"Press the attack!" Jorb ordered his trainee.

Bill lunged forward, frustrated by the spiral of paper that kept getting in the way of his slashes, and Julie tripped over her own feet while getting out of the way. As she swung her arms wildly trying to maintain her balance, her own paper blade caught Bill's extended arm in the crook of the elbow.

"First touch," the bunny crowed, hopping between the combatants and casually deflecting their instinctual attacks with his own practice weapon. "Swords down."

"I won?" Julie asked.

"You took his arm off," the Drazen told her. "At least you would have if you were fighting with real swords."

"Here," Bill said, offering to return his now-scrolled paper roll to Jorb, handle-first.

"You keep it. You too, Julie. Practice the forms with each other if you have time, but no sparring without either myself or the director present or you'll just teach each other bad habits."

"I hope we won't all be sword fighting," Harry spoke up from the front-row seat he had taken. "I'm a little old for that much jumping around."

"As director, I'll be making all of the casting decisions," the Grenouthian said, counting the newcomers with a furry finger. "Everybody appears to have found their way here, which is more than I can say for my last class. Now, how many of you have had some theatrical training?"

"Harry and I acted in college productions," Irene announced.

"Excellent. I want you to forget whatever you think you learned. Anybody else?" Not surprisingly, none of the other aspiring actors spoke up. "Even better. How many of you would class yourselves as expert with a sword? No? Intermediate?" The bunny's head slumped towards his chest, and he croaked, "Beginner?"

"Where would we have learned sword fighting?" Harry asked. "It's archaic."

"How could you do Shakespeare without swords? Did your college cut out the fight scenes for fear of offending the tender sensitivities of the students?"

"We didn't do Shakespeare."

"But I specifically asked if you had theatrical training."

"Which you told us to forget," Harry retorted. "Besides, Shakespeare isn't the only human playwright."

"He is in my book," the Grenouthian shot back. "Very well, you can all learn your lines first and I'll choreograph the fight scenes later. Maybe I'll bring in some ringers from the other species if Flower allows it. Think you can keep your tentacle under wraps for a whole performance, Jorb?"

"He's got too many fingers for a human," Harry pointed out.

"It's better than too few," the Drazen said. "I can fold one of my thumbs in and wear gloves."

"Maybe we could do a different production," somebody suggested. "I took a book of plays from the twenty-first century out from the library to prepare for this and some of them weren't that bad."

"Over my dead body," the director declared, flicking his wrist to redeploy the paper sword.

"Drama queen," Flower commented in Julie's head. "But he really is a good director. The whole theatre company was his idea."

"Do you have scripts to give us?" Irene asked.

"For Shakespeare?" the director asked incredulously. "I know for a fact that his collected works are included with the free dictionaries on every one of those cheap tabs you all carry around to read the newspaper."

"I didn't bring my tab."

"Neither did I," another student volunteered.

"Haven't you ever heard of sharing?" the Grenouthian demanded.

"I don't own a tab," Bill confessed.

"Me neither," Julie added hastily. "I have a teacher bot back in my cabin, though, and it has Shakespeare's works."

"How many of you have a tab with you?" the director asked. "Show of hands. I see," he continued when only two of the humans responded in the affirmative. "I would have preferred assigning parts and doing my initial assessments based on a cold reading, but instead I'll have you take turns offering monologues. Would those of you who came prepared please open to Hamlet, Act Three, Scene Three, for the famous monologue."

"To be or not to—" a young man who didn't have a tab began, only to be cut off by a growl from the Grenouthian.

"Not that monologue. This speech belongs to Claudius, and begins, 'Oh, my offence is rank,' which I have no doubt sums up your acting abilities."

"Found it," one woman who had brought a tab said a second before the other.

"Excellent. Bill, you go first."

"What?" the young man said.

"Just take the tab and do it quickly before you have time to get nervous," the Grenouthian told him, not unkindly. "Just read the lines, don't try to act."

Bill accepted the tab, though holding it up, it was obvious that his hand was trembling. He let out a sort of a croak, cleared his throat, and then began:

Oh, my offence is rank. It smells to heaven.
It hath the primal eldest curse upon 't,
A brother's murder.

"Enough," the director stopped him. "Give the tab to Julie."

"Why me?" the girl asked. "I remember this play and it's a boy's part."

"No. When Shakespeare wrote these plays the women's parts were acted by boys. Claudius is definitely a man's part."

"But I'm a woman!"

"And how many women do you see here? You can't all be Ophelia and Gertrude, you know. Just read it."

Oh, my offence is rank. It smells to heaven.
It hath the primal eldest curse upon 't,
A brother's murder. Pray can I not.
Though inclination be as sharp as will,
My stronger guilt defeats my strong intent,
And, like a man to double business bound,
I stand in pause where I shall first begin,
And both neglect. What if this cursèd hand

"Stop," the bunny interrupted her. "Ladies and gentlemen, I believe we have our Claudius."

Sixteen

"That habitat must be even bigger than Flower," Dave marveled, as the shuttle carrying all thirty-nine members of the independent living cooperative approached the Alfe recycling facility. Everybody was staring at the hologram of their destination, which floated at the front of the shuttle's passenger cabin. "Look at the size of that opening."

"The recycling center is just a giant empty cylinder with a few residential decks wrapped around the outside," Lynx told them. "It's owned by the Sharf, but so many humans work here that they've been allowed to establish their own government and join the Conference of Sovereign Human Communities. We've stopped here every circuit and it's always been profitable for all parties concerned."

"So what do they recycle here?" Harry asked.

"Hulks of ships that aren't worth renovating after so many years of service, derelict space factories, damaged cargo containers. Anything with enough metal to make it worthwhile. This star system is centrally located in the sector and there's a tunnel network connection, so it's cheap enough to push, pull or tow the wrecks here. The Stryx offer a deep discount on tunnel tolls for recycling which makes it cost efficient to bring junk from halfway across the galaxy."

"How did so many humans get jobs here?" Nancy asked.

"The Sharf originally recruited them off Earth, I suppose. Even with all of the safety precautions the aliens put in place, it's still dangerous work. Cutting apart old wrecks is the sort of job that usually falls to the new kids on the block."

"They won't switch over to full automation as long as they can find some species willing to do the work," the former teacher concluded.

"That's right, and it pays better than most contract labor jobs. Some of the humans working here are the third generation, and the recycling habitat is the only home they've ever known."

"So we're going to enter the center of the cylinder and take a lift tube to the residential decks, like on Flower?" Irene asked.

"No, it's too dangerous to mix civilian traffic and junk in the core. Flower will match the shuttle's radial velocity to a hangar on the outer deck and we'll be at around ninety percent of Earth gravity when we dock. The spin rate is a compromise between the humans and the Sharf who still live here."

Even as Lynx spoke, the acceleration chairs on the shuttle all swung to an odd angle that compensated for a course change, and the thrust pushed the passengers gently back in their seats. Conversation fell off as everyone's eyes were glued to the hologram that seemed to show the habitat's rate of spin slowing as their transport approached an impossibly small opening. When the Dollnick AI neatly inserted the shuttle into the hangar, the senior citizens broke out in applause.

"Simple mathematics," Flower said over Lynx's implant, but the third officer was sure she detected a bit of self-satisfaction in the AI's tone before the voice shifted to the public address system. "Please remain in your seats with your safety harnesses buckled until the hangar operator extends the airlock. For some reason that defies logic, the Sharf on this habitat are resistant to using atmosphere retention fields in visitor areas."

A minute later, the shuttle passengers felt a gentle lurch, and then the hatch hissed open, revealing a tube surrounded by accordion-like folds of some alien fabric. Everybody removed their safety harnesses and followed Lynx through the connecting tube into a large airlock. Once they were all inside, the outer door closed, and a moment later, the inner door opened on what appeared to be a pedestrian mall, complete with palm trees.

"I'll meet you all back here in eight hours when Flower returns the shuttle," Lynx announced. "I have to see the habitat manager about some business, but good luck with your plans, and don't work too hard."

"Thank you," Jack said. He extended both arms like a policeman holding back a crowd to prevent his fellow retirees from scattering. "Listen up, people. I know we already went over this in the shuttle, but some of us have minor issues with our short term memory so it won't hurt to do a brief review. Now, who doesn't have flyers?"

"I don't," Irene said.

"That's because you're our official camera person, and don't break it, or the Grenouthian will kill us," Harry reminded her.

"We aren't going to use footage of handing out flyers in a commercial," she protested. "That would look like we were running some kind of forced labor camp for senior citizens."

"I'll be taking still images to go with my story in the Galactic Free Press," Dianne spoke up. "If you want to use any of them in your advertising later, the paper offers generous licensing terms as long as you give proper attribution."

"And we all owe Dianne our thanks for making her husband print up these flyers for us," Jack said. "I don't think anybody else aboard Flower could have done it."

"The flyers should be a real attention-getter," Nancy concurred. "I imagine that many of the people who grew up here have never even seen single sheets of paper."

"Do not take off the bracelets that Lynx gave us on the shuttle," Jack continued. "If any of us should have a senior moment and get lost, the bracelets allow Flower to locate us and report our locations. But that's a last resort, so let's stick with the buddy system and nobody goes wandering off on their own."

"Do we have to give away all of our flyers before we can eat?" somebody asked.

"Just do your best. I do hope we can finish before lunch so that Irene can get plenty of footage of us visiting the attractions and having a good time. How many independent living facilities on Earth can run commercials showing their residents visiting places all over the galaxy?"

With that, the group broke up, and the pre-assigned pairs began spreading out through the mall to put some distance between the teams before they started accosting the locals. Irene and Harry found themselves strolling through a small plaza with a number of fixed-in-place metal tables featuring chess boards or other game grids embossed on the surface. The seats were taken almost exclusively by older people.

"Bingo," Harry muttered, but then he let out a reluctant sigh. "I can't believe I let you talk me into doing this."

"You'll be fine," Irene said. "You're better at talking to people than you realize. I want to practice with the camera a little, but if you're really uncomfortable recruiting new members, I'll take over as soon as I learn the basic controls. I need to get used to the fact that it floats on its own."

"That's the only way they can completely eliminate the vibrations so that different camera angles can be combined for 3D," her husband said while fishing a couple of flyers from his satchel. "The bunny claimed that it's actually a professional studio camera, but when you only use one of them, the result isn't that different than flat video."

"As long as it works. Go try your pitch on the woman with the knitting."

"I want to start with somebody who isn't armed with foot-long needles."

"What a big baby. So talk to the man who's sitting alone stacking checkers."

Harry grunted and walked over to a table where a man a few years older than himself was fidgeting with black and red checkers.

"Game?" the man inquired.

"Actually, I wanted to talk to you about—"

"Talk while we play," the man interrupted, shoving the red checkers across the board to Harry. "Who's the woman pointing that thing at us?"

"My wife, and it's a Grenouthian camera. She's practicing to make a commercial for our—"

"Come on, put them on the dark squares," the man cut Harry off impatiently. He quickly arranged his own pieces and then advanced one on a diagonal. "Black moves first. What's the matter? Haven't you played draughts before?"

"I've played checkers," Harry said. He felt his temper rising but was unwilling to quit on his first attempt to give away a flyer, especially with his wife recording it for posterity. "I'd like to talk to you about—"

"Your move," the man interrupted again. "You must be from the Yankee side of the globe to call this game checkers. New here? You look a bit old to be starting a career in recycling."

"I'm retired," Harry said, trying to keep up with the other player's rapid moves. "I'm with the independent living cooperative on Flower. Take this," he added, offering a flyer.

"Take that!" his opponent crowed, jumping two of Harry's men and removing them from the board. The action must have improved his mood because he accepted the sheet of paper. "Why would I want to have my knees resurfaced? There's nothing wrong with them."

"Turn it over," Harry said, trying to puzzle out a place he could move without losing a man. He finally realized that he could jump the attacking piece, but this led to a rapid exchange, and before he knew it, his opponent had a king and was attacking from the rear. "I haven't played in almost sixty years."

"It shows," his opponent said, barely even glancing at the board to counter Harry's increasingly desperate moves. "Is this for real, then?"

"We've formed an independent living cooperative, and as a professional baker for over forty years, I can assure you that the food is better than what you get in a restaurant."

"I meant the prices. Two hundred and fifty creds a cycle covers the room?"

"And includes the professional management fee." The cooperative members had argued late into the night over how much they should mark up Flower's basic room charge, but in the end, the newcomer from Break Rock settled it by telling them that if the rate was too cheap, nobody would believe it. "Everything else is a-la-carte."

"It sounds like living on a cruise ship," the man said as he casually removed Harry's last piece from the board. "I've always wanted to see more of the galaxy. Where have you been so far?"

"Uh, Break Rock, and here, but I didn't get off at Break Rock. I only left Earth a few weeks ago. Eccentric Enterprises and Flower have been running the circuit for years, but we're just launching our independent living cooperative."

"I've been aboard Flower every time she's stopped here," the man said, putting down the flyer and extending his hand across the table. "I'm Tom."

"Harry, and that's Irene with the camera."

"You're saying there's no long-term commitment?"

"You can rent by the cycle," Harry confirmed. "If you'd rather go by months, I think it's only a hundred and fifty creds for the room, but Flower will charge a cleaning fee if you leave before the end of the cycle."

"That's half of what I'm paying here," Tom admitted, poking his finger at the list of activities on the flyer. "Do you really do all this stuff?"

"Yes. Well, some of it is kind of required by Flower, like the calisthenics and the team sport. I'm actually working part-time in one of her kitchens to make some extra money. We haven't gone on many group outings yet because we just started, but we're planning on a field trip everywhere we stop from now on."

"Will I have to hand out flyers?" Tom asked.

"It's optional. We're all new at this, as you can probably tell, so you have a chance to get in on the ground floor." Harry winced when he realized he had repeated part of the sales pitch that had tricked him into leaving Earth in the first place. "I had friends back on the mother world who signed up for independent living and they all complained about the food after the first couple weeks. I guarantee that's not going to happen on Flower, and pretty much all of the food is grown on board."

"The food's decent here, but there's a limited menu unless you can afford the restaurants, which is a once-a-week thing for me. When is this open house? I don't really bother keeping track of the date anymore."

"It's tomorrow. Bring your luggage and you can move right in if you like it."

"You'll find that most of the retirees here have families they won't want to leave," Tom cautioned. "My own wife went back to Earth a couple years after we moved out here and I never remarried. Hey," he said in a lower voice while glancing at Irene, who was now focused on a pair of chess players. "Any single ladies in this independent living cooperative of yours?"

"It's around fifty-fifty, couples versus singles," Harry estimated. "And from what I've seen, there are plenty more women our age living on Flower with their children or by themselves on the residential decks. Our next marketing push is going to be to them."

Tom nodded. "You'll see me at the open house. Do I have to sign something so you can make your quota?"

"That wouldn't have been a bad idea but we didn't think of it," Harry said, rising from the table. "What are my chances with the woman over there who's knitting?"

"Martha? Those are baby socks she's working on but you can give it a try. Maybe she's tired of changing diapers."

Harry approached the grandmother, whose flying needles were clicking so rapidly that they reminded him of an old wind-up timer he'd used for years in his kitchen. He waited for her to stop and look at him questioningly before offering her a flyer.

"There's nothing wrong with my knees, thank you," Martha told him after glancing at the advertisement.

"Sorry, I gave it to you wrong side up," Harry apologized. "I'm talking to people about the new independent living cooperative on Flower and Tom said I might try you."

"That old coot?" She turned over the flyer and skimmed the text while adding, "The women in your independent living cooperative will have their hands full if you let him join."

"We've got a great group of people and we've only just started, so you'll have a chance to shape your own future," Harry said, wondering at his newfound loquacity as the words flowed from his mouth. Back on Earth, Irene had handled all of their customer service. "This recycling center is a regular stop on the circuit so you'd be back here every six months without having to make a special trip."

"Or, I could wait six months to see how things shape up and join you when my granddaughter is ready for nursery school," Martha said. "Is there a limit to how many people you're taking?"

"You know, we've never discussed that," Harry admitted. "It's not like we have to build rooms if we get more people. Flower has over a million empty cabins and she could handle all of the food services and cleaning herself if she wanted to."

"Flower?"

"The Dollnick AI who runs the ship. She seems really keen on getting more people on board, something about the economies of scale."

"Well, I'll come to your open house out of curiosity, but I'm not making any moves for at least another six months."

After his first two contacts had not only accepted flyers but promised to come to the open house, Harry found it a bit of a letdown that he didn't get any more bites before lunch. When he and Irene reached the food court area of the pedestrian mall and found their group, he was surprised to learn that some of the teams had given up without getting a single positive response. Dave, on the other hand, had gotten five firm commitments to the open house and sold three knee-joint-resurfacing jobs for the Farling doctor.

"I never thought I'd be dropping my pants in front of an audience but they insisted on seeing the puncture mark where the needle went in," Dave explained. "It's going to be a problem if we do this again at the next stop because the scar will be completely healed by then."

"Is the doctor paying you commission?" Harry asked.

"No, but he covered half of the printing cost for our flyers. You have to admit that having an alien super-doctor on the staff is a pretty big bonus for an independent living facility."

"He's on our staff?"

Dave shrugged. "I asked him if we could use his name and he said it's no chitin off his carapace."

"When I discussed the flyer with the doctor, he told me that old people are good for business and we should try to find some sick ones," Nancy said. Then her eyes went round and she pointed wordlessly at one of the enormous displays that graced the walls of the food court. The close-captioned version of the Grenouthian tunnel network news had gone to commercial, and the video showed a close-up of Harry in ecstasy after tasting Flower's bread.

"That's you," Irene said unnecessarily, poking her husband in the side. The scene shifted to a shirtless Jack rowing a one-man scull on the reservoir deck, and from there, to Nancy reading a book to a group of angelic children. Next there was a long shot of Dave limping painfully into the Farling doctor's clinic, then emerging and doing a few dance steps as soon as the door closed behind him.

"Did you do this as a surprise?" Harry asked his wife when the video cut to a shot showing a group of women, including Irene, on a shopping outing to the bazaar. "If not you, who—"

"The Independent Living Cooperative on Flower," his wife read as English text began scrolling across the bottom of the video, which had cut to showing all of the members eating together in the common room. "Now accepting applications for furnished suites starting at two-hundred and fifty creds a cycle. You don't have to be alone anymore. Come to our open house all day tomorrow. Validated shuttle tickets on request."

"This has to be Flower's doing," Jack surmised. "She must be getting video from those bots of hers."

"She's obviously trying to help, though I wish she had consulted with us first," Nancy said. "I wonder how much she's paying to rent time on the displays."

"Excuse me," a well-dressed man in his middle years addressed them. "I couldn't help recognizing some of you from that commercial. Are you all here from Flower?"

"That's right," Jack said. "I'm afraid we have an age cut-off though, and you aren't old enough."

"If I could just take a minute of your time," the man continued, producing a flat coin purse with a flexible video display on one side. "My cousin is traveling on Flower and she was supposed to meet me here." The display came to life, showing a picture of a young woman. "Do any of you recognize her?"

"That's Julie," Irene identified the image immediately. "She's on our theatre team."

"Julie," the man repeated, his face stretching into a broad smile that exposed a number of gold teeth. "That's right. How often do you have rehearsals?"

"Every evening when the ship is underway, but all of the team sports are on hold while we're at a stop."

"That's perfect. I mean, if she doesn't show up in the next day or two I'll just pop over and hunt her down. Thank you very much."

"Do you have your ear-cuff translator with you, Jack?" Nancy asked as soon as the man headed off.

"No. I didn't expect to talk with any aliens here. What did you want it for?"

"I was going to try to contact Flower," the former teacher said apprehensively. "I volunteer in the library where Julie interns and she told me she doesn't have any family."

"Julie probably meant immediate family," Irene said, though she was obviously troubled by Nancy's words.

"Oh, here comes the Galactic Free Press reporter. Maybe she'll know how to contact Flower."

"Big smiles, everyone," Dianne said, stopping a few paces away to take a picture. "What's the matter? Isn't anybody taking your flyers?"

"I suspect we'll have more guests at our open house than we can handle, thanks to Flower running her own commercial on the public displays here," Jack said. "We're feeling a little uncomfortable because somebody claiming to be related to a young woman on board just showed us a picture of her which Irene confirmed. Nancy says the girl has no family."

"Are you talking about Julie?" the reporter asked immediately.

"How did you know?"

"It's probably nothing to worry about," Dianne said, ignoring the question. "I have a high grade implant and I can raise Flower from here if she's listening." The reporter stood rigid for a moment, her eyes focused on something the others couldn't see, and then she relaxed. "Do you have a description?"

"Middle aged, black hair, gold teeth. He was wearing an expensive suit," Irene added. "I think it was designer."

"My wife and her fashions," Harry grumbled.

Dianne grew still for another moment, and then she said, "I've passed your information along and Flower said to tell you that everything is under control."

Seventeen

"We're supposed to be undercover," an impossibly beautiful Vergallian woman complained. "Gathering us all in the same room for the sake of a briefing is extraordinarily irresponsible tradecraft. I would have thought your Drazen allies would have taught you that much."

"I asked you all here because Flower and I believe that you can help us," Woojin said. "Access to this cafeteria is limited to invited guests and ship's officers."

"Get on with it then," the giant bunny demanded. "Time is creds, and I was on my way to see about some props when Flower hijacked the lift tube capsule and brought me here without an explanation. I was afraid it would be another one of her exercise manias."

"I smell another bonus coming my way," the station head of Dollnick intelligence boasted, leaning back in his chair and cracking the knuckles on all four of his hands simultaneously.

"Thank you for bringing that up, Lume," Woojin said. "As it happens, Flower is willing to compensate all of you at above industry standard rates for your help. But first, I have to ask that you will keep what I tell you in complete confidence."

A dozen alien spies burst out laughing, stamping their feet, patting their bellies, and otherwise displaying their mirth at the captain's request. Even Flower let out an untranslatable whistle of amusement over the room's speakers.

"I'm sure he didn't mean from our employers," Lume assured the others when he'd recovered his breath. "Humanese is an inexact language."

Woojin self-consciously adjusted the three-cornered hat which Flower had insisted he don in return for compelling the alien agents to show up for the meeting. "In cooperation with EarthCent Intelligence, our civil authorities back on Earth have been cracking down on organized crime, especially drug gangs affiliated with alien smugglers. Their first major success—"

"Is this about Julie?" the Vergallian agent interrupted.

"Uh, yes. Let me explain to the others in case—"

"Oh, we know all about her," the Grenouthian said. "She testified against the bosses of your top syndicate and in return you gave her a part-time job in a library that pays so poorly she has to supplement her income waiting tables at *The Spoon*. How do you expect to recruit more whistleblowers back on Earth when they hear how you've treated her?"

"She's the first person in our witness protection program and we're still fine-tuning," Woojin protested. "Is there anybody in this room who doesn't know as much about Julie as I do?"

"I just got a message from the home office that there's a million cred contract out on the young lady," Razood contributed. "My understanding is that it's prepaid, so a neutral pirate group is already holding the money.

"Can your people compel the pirates to return the money and have the contract cancelled?"

"I don't think so," the Frunge blacksmith replied, "but I'm fairly new to the intelligence business myself so I don't know much about how these things play out."

"The Assassins Guild doesn't work on credit," Lume said, and the Grenouthian spy grunted his agreement. "It's cash payment upfront, and the contract is open to any supplier."

"And thanks to the marvelous security around here, I'll bet that every professional killer in the galaxy knows exactly where the target is living," the Vergallian pointed out unhelpfully.

"I already said that we're new at witness protection," Woojin shot back in irritation. "What I'm asking for—what Flower and I are asking for—is your cooperation in keeping Julie safe."

"And what does the young lady have to say about all of this?" Jorb asked, tapping his head thoughtfully with his tentacle.

"We haven't had that conversation. Julie obviously knows that her former employers want her dead, but telling her that there's a million cred price on her head would just be cruel."

"Well, it should be easy enough to protect her," Lume said cheerfully. "Flower can keep an eye on the girl around the clock and watch for known assassins boarding at our stops. I'm sure my colleagues will be as pleased as I am by this opportunity to keep our skills sharp and earn bonuses."

"Couldn't you just assign a couple of bots to follow her around at a discreet distance?" the Drazen inquired.

"She's too observant, Jorb," Flower answered. "Although I haven't seen any mention of it in their technical specifications, some members of the Human species seem to have a sixth sense about being followed."

"Technical specifications?" Woojin asked.

"*Humans for Aliens,*" Lume told him. "A fascinating read. It's quite broad-minded of your people to publish such a useful manual that describes how you operate. It's filled in quite a few holes for the rest of us."

"At great savings to our intelligence service," the Grenouthian agreed. "I have credible information that it was actually ghost written by a Stryx."

An alien who might have passed as human in bad lighting cleared her throat.

"Yes, Spy Gem?" Woojin asked the clone.

"I just want to state for the record that the nanobots the Farling doctor removed from your witness were purchased from rogue Gem who work with the pirates. Our legitimate retail channels have only sold surveillance nanobots since our revolution."

"I never suspected otherwise."

"The assassins don't seem to be having any difficulty locating the girl," Lume observed.

"The one who followed her to the water deck may have been consulting some sort of tracking device, but that was before the Farling operated to remove the nanobots," Flower informed them. "I'm increasing the number of surveillance cameras in the main entry points and I've activated a number of bots to act as extra eyes."

"Where's the device now?" the clone asked. "If it's Gem technology, I might be able to learn something."

"It was in the form of a wearable device so I'm afraid it was eaten along with its owner."

Lume burst out laughing. "You lured an assassin onto the water deck and had one of your pet fish eat him?"

"It seemed like a good idea at the time," Flower said modestly.

"It seems unlikely that a contract killer was hanging around the Sharf recycling center waiting for an assignment," Woojin continued. "Thanks to the alertness of one of the seniors in our new independent living section, we have a pretty good description of the killer. My worry is that there may be more."

"You need to stamp out the problem at its source," the Farling rubbed out on his speaking legs. "I've already repaired that girl once and I won't have a bunch of hired killers messing up my work."

"Why are you here?" the Grenouthian asked. "You're not even with an intelligence service. You're an outcast."

"Flower invited me, and I prefer to think of myself as idiosyncratic. I've dabbled in spying over the years and I encountered a similar situation once back before any of you were born, hatched, or grown in a vat. It involved a revenge killing arranged for by the family members of a particularly nasty criminal who had none the less been very good at sending money to his mother. You know the type."

A chorus of assents met the giant beetle's statement.

"The bounty hunter who had taken out this piece of trash found herself targeted by killers from half the galaxy after the family placed a large price on her head. She was a valuable source of information for an operation I was running at the time so I arranged for a reverse contract through the Tharks."

"You paid the Tharks to undo the contract?" Woojin asked.

"Not a contract reversal, a reverse contract," the doctor explained. "It cost me ten percent of the contract value to have the Tharks make odds that anybody who got to my bounty hunter would themselves be killed within a cycle."

"You mean, if she had been assassinated, the killer would have been signing his own death warrant," Lume surmised. "Interesting. And it only cost you ten percent?"

"It's a gamble," the beetle explained. "If the bookie had to put his clan to the bother of tracking down and eliminating a killer they might have lost money, but the criminal element is terrified of incurring the wrath of the Tharks, especially since they handle so much of the dark money in the galaxy. The bookie takes all of that into account when he makes the odds."

"Ten percent of a million is a hundred thousand," Woojin said, leading to a sarcastic round of applause from the aliens at his display of mathematical acumen. "I'll contact Earth, but I don't know if they'll be willing to pay."

"That's only half the problem. One of the reasons the original contract went unfilled is because the bounty hunter took the precaution of eliminating the family members who had placed it. That's what I meant about stamping out these problems at their source."

"You're suggesting that we execute the leaders of the drug syndicate?"

"You should do that anyway just as a matter of good housekeeping," the bunny commented. "I have to get back to the theatre but I'll check with my sources about the contract and let you know what I find out. Will the lift tube operate properly now, Flower?"

"Yes, but you're missing out on a new dessert I'm trying from the tunnel network all-species cookbook. I have a few part-timers working in this kitchen now."

"Since when is there an all-species cookbook?" Woojin asked.

"All species except humans," Flower corrected herself. "The latest edition came out a few thousand years ago. It's not very popular because the recipes require a mix of ingredients that won't kill any of the advanced species."

"Is this going to be another one of those vegan treats that taste like sawdust?" Jorb made a face and got up from his place. "Who wants food made from the lowest common denominator? I'd rather eat out of the trashcan."

"No, this one is supposed to be very good," Flower insisted. "In fact, it may be too hot for you."

Nobody was surprised when Jorb sat right back down again and glared at the overhead speaker grille. The Drazens were famous for relishing hot peppers that other species were more inclined to weaponize for crowd control. Lume went over to the bar and began mixing drinks for the other spies in showy fashion that employed all four of his hands, while Woojin tried teasing some details about the Farling's past out of the doctor without success.

"Ta dah," Flower announced, as Bill entered the cafeteria through the swinging door, his head turned as far away as possible from the tray he was carrying. The young man's face was bright red and sweat was starting to glisten in his hair. He practically threw the tray down on the table and then rushed over to the bar and ran his face under the faucet.

The collected spies all watched cautiously as Jorb helped himself to one of the pastries which featured translucent dough of some sort wrapped around a pulpy filling. "Not bad," he wheezed. "You should try it, Lume."

All of the other aliens present took one look at the tears flowing from the Drazen's eyes, downed their drinks, and with the exception of the doctor, fled for the exit.

"Maybe I shouldn't have told Harry to add a whole bottle of hot sauce," Flower mused. "The recipe only called for a dash, but I was worried it would be too bland."

Woojin went to check on Bill, who had submerged his whole head in the bar sink, which was now half full of water. The beetle looked up from the cursory examination he was giving the Drazen spy, who seemed to be having difficulty breathing. "Tell the boy not to rub his eyes," the doctor called over to Woojin, "and use plenty of soap."

"Oh, that's good," Jorb croaked, thumping his chest with his fist while patting his own back with his tentacle. "It starts with fruity overtones and finishes like boiling lead. Can I take these to go?"

"Help yourself," Flower said. "I'll give your compliments to the chef."

"If he's still alive," the beetle added pessimistically as he headed for the kitchen. "Humans aren't rated to work with the ingredients in the all-species cookbook."

Bill finally came up for air as the doctor disappeared through the swinging door. "Captain? I didn't eat any, I swear. I just didn't see the point of putting on rubber gloves to wash up."

"Now?"

"In the kitchen. The baker said that the dessert was supposed to air for a few minutes before serving so I offered to wash the pots and pans. This is my first shift working as a waiter and I wanted to show that I'm not too stuck up to do dishes."

"Are you alright now?"

"I think so, but I'm wearing goggles the next time Flower says that something might be a little hot. I thought she meant the water." Bill blinked his eyes rapidly and found that he was no longer crying. "It didn't seem to bother Harry at all."

"Is that the baker? Maybe he's having a delayed reaction. I'll go check on him."

When Woojin entered the kitchen, he was amused to find the Farling standing still with all of his appendages folded across the belly of his carapace. Harry was backed up against the counter brandishing a chef's knife to keep the alien at bay.

"This one sets a new bar for bad patients," the beetle remarked to the captain. "I considered disarming him, but it doesn't look like he requires treatment, and I was afraid of unintentionally bringing about a cardiac episode and then having to carry him all the way back to my clinic."

"You're the doctor?" Harry demanded, lowering the knife. "Why didn't you say so?"

"I asked if you were damaged in any way."

"I thought you were probing for a weakness, like a predator picking out the sick animal in the herd."

"M793qK is the best doctor who's ever worked on me, and as a former mercenary, I've been patched up quite a few times over the years," Woojin informed the baker. "Why don't we all have a seat in the cafeteria so I can bring you and Bill up to speed on working here."

"You're responsible for alien food service?" Harry asked. He put down the knife and followed the beetle and Woojin back out to the dining room.

"Come over here and sit down, Bill," the captain summoned the young man, who was still standing uncertainly behind the bar. Jorb and the tray of desserts had disappeared.

"Yes, sir," Bill said. "Am I in trouble?"

"I want to speak to you both about your new jobs," the captain said. "I assume Flower has informed you that this cafeteria is frequented by the unattached aliens on board."

"She said they eat together for the company," Harry confirmed. "I've only cooked a few meals so far, mainly baking. It's all new to me, being alien recipes, but it's interesting."

"What I'm about to tell you has to remain confidential, and I want you both to give me your word that it won't leave this room. What's so funny?" Woojin addressed the beetle, who was rubbing out the Farling equivalent of a gale of laughter on his speaking legs.

"Humans and their little secrets."

The captain turned his body as if to exclude the doctor from the conversation before continuing. "The two of you agree?"

"Yes, Captain," Bill said.

"I'd have to hear what you say first," Harry replied. "And my wife says I talk in my sleep, though I suspect she stays awake just to ask me questions while my defences are down."

"I suppose nothing on this ship ever stays secret for long anyway," Woojin grumbled. "Most of the aliens who come here to eat are intelligence agents."

"We have alien spies working for us?" the baker asked.

M793qK, who had been leaning over a chair on the belly of his carapace, slid to the deck and seemed to go into convulsions.

"I'm glad we're able to amuse you," Woojin said in the doctor's direction. "No, Harry. The spies work for the various intelligence agencies run by their species. They're here through an agreement with EarthCent Intelligence."

"I don't get it. We're taking a bunch of alien spies around to all of the sovereign human communities?"

"It saves them a lot of money they would spend on field agents otherwise and they pay us the difference," Woojin explained. "It takes a lot of income to keep a ship this large going, and this way we can keep an eye on them and build interagency relations."

"Does this mean that you're some sort of spy too?" Bill asked.

"Former spy," the captain said, which was only a half-lie. "Whatever the good doctor believes about our ability to keep secrets, the truth is that the alien agents on board are the least discreet bunch I've ever seen in my life. I suspect it's because they don't take us seriously."

"Do you mean that Razood is a spy too? He's not even that old," Bill protested. "He told me that running the smithy in Colonial Jeevesburg is his first real job."

"Razood and a few of the others are on their first assignment. They were recruited for intelligence work because they signed onto Flower to pursue their chosen professions, but that doesn't mean they aren't tough customers, especially the bunny."

Eighteen

"Do you know where you're going?" Julie asked Bill as he led her through a maze of vendors selling everything from footwear to holographic entertainment systems. "I swear you're taking turns at random."

"This is the shortest way to Colonial Jeevesburg. I'll introduce you to Razood."

"And he's really willing to loan us practice swords?"

"When I showed him the paper swords that Jorb gave us he actually got angry and said something about nailing a tentacle to the wall," Bill explained. "Apparently the Frunge take swordsmanship more seriously than the Drazens."

"I'm surprised that any of the advanced species still play around with edged weapons. Flower nagged me into shopping here yesterday and the Dollnick merchant she recommended sold me this disposable stunner." She fished in her purse and brought out a nasty looking hand-weapon. "He said as long as I leave the dial on the blue side of the scale it won't kill anybody."

"Disposable stunners only have one setting—stun," Bill said. "Razood has a whole library of alien weapons on his tab that I'm supposed to study when I'm on break and that looks to me like Dolly military issue."

"Do you think I've bought stolen goods?" Julie asked.

"What did it cost you?"

"Five creds."

"Something's wrong," Bill told her. "I don't know a lot about weapons but I think five thousand creds would probably make more sense."

"That's more than I could make in a year!"

"Yeah. The good stuff isn't cheap. Remember I told you that I got recruited by a gang on Break Rock? I asked if anybody had any serious weapons, like the ones you see on the alien holo-channels. The guy who was supposed to be my trainer just laughed at me and said that if he could afford anything like that he wouldn't be mugging drunk miners for a living."

"Aren't there any laws about weapons on board?"

"I don't know. The security chief told me that Flower has enough of her own military hardware that she could take over a star system if she wanted. Do you mind if I ask Razood about your stunner?"

"I guess not," Julie said, and then attempted to contact the ship's AI through the subvocalization pickup for her implant. "Flower?"

"Yes, Julie."

"I bought a stunner from the Dollnick with the weapons stall that you suggested, but I just showed it to Bill and he thinks it's actually military issue."

"I can't believe Zube would make a mistake," the AI replied. "Just hold onto it for now."

"Are you okay?" Bill asked. "You're kind of mumbling and your lips are moving."

"Sorry, I was talking to Flower over my implant. I'm still getting used to it."

"I wish I could afford one. I almost lost my ear-cuff translator sticking my head in a sink this afternoon. It's a good thing they're waterproof."

"Why'd you do that?"

"Long story," Bill said, remembering that he'd promised the captain not to talk about the alien intelligence agents. "There's Razood's smithy."

The Frunge blacksmith had his back turned and was hammering a red-hot chunk of iron on his anvil as they approached. Julie stopped at the large display table to admire the swords, and after a few seconds of dividing her attention between the blades and Razood, she figured out what was bothering her.

"Why isn't it louder?"

"Oh, there's a noise suppression field," Bill said. "Razood hates using it but the other exhibitors complain if he doesn't. When we're between stops and there's less pedestrian traffic, he turns it off and you can hear the clangs all the way to the food court."

"So that's what it was. Sometimes I think I hear a bell ringing in the distance while I'm waiting tables at *The Spoon,* but I didn't want to ask in case nobody else could hear it."

"Yeah, it doesn't pay to stand out."

"Did your boss make all of those weapons?" Julie asked.

"Some of them came in for repairs. This one's my favorite," Bill said, hefting a long broadsword with a hilt that was obviously intended for two hands. "It's a Horten berserker sword."

"Jorb said something about berserkers the other day, but I thought they all used axes."

"Razood says that Drazens are axe-happy." The apprentice took an experimental swing with the sword, pulling himself off balance and almost stumbling.

"Careful," Razood barked over his shoulder. "That sword is worth more than you are."

"How did he even see you?" Julie asked as the blacksmith went back to hammering away at the work on the anvil.

"I don't know," Bill admitted. "He always seems to know what's going on around him. He says it's because the Frunge day has more hours than ours so it seems to him like we're standing still half of the time."

"That doesn't make any sense."

"I didn't think so either."

There was a loud hiss as the blacksmith quenched a proto-blade in a bucket of water.

"Anything I can do to help, boss?" Bill asked.

"You're not back on the clock until tomorrow morning, your time," the Frunge replied. "I won't have it said that I abuse my apprentices. Is this the young lady you're always talking about?"

"He's exaggerating," Bill rushed to tell Julie, and the tips of his ears turned pink. "We're here about those practice swords."

"Ah, yes. The Drazen would have you play with children's toys. I have a matched set of rapiers that I could let you use, though I should weld buttons on the tips first. Or there are a couple of claymores from Earth with nice basket hilts that I got from Flower's lost-and-found."

"You claimed them from the lost-and-found even though they weren't yours?" Julie asked.

"Flower has her own notions of how such things should work. Her legal position is that if you abandon any property in a public area for more than a standard sleep/wake cycle for your species, it becomes unclaimed property and she sells it."

"Just one day?"

"Finders keepers," the AI commented over the girl's implant. "If people want a nanny, they can move to a Stryx station."

"And what about the rapiers?" Bill asked.

"They came in for repairs during our first circuit. Three years is too long for a member of your species to abandon property in a blacksmith's shop. That's my legal position."

"Rapiers are the skinny blades?" Julie asked.

"That's one way of putting it," Razood said. "I much prefer the claymores myself."

The Frunge grabbed the hilt of a sword that was stuck in a barrel with at least fifty other weapons, pulled it out with a flourish, then gripped the blade with his other hand and presented it to Julie, hilt-first. Her hand seemed to be swallowed up by the basket protecting the grip area, but the sword was well balanced.

"It's not as heavy as it looks," she said, making a few experimental thrusts and parries.

"Wait until you've been swinging it around for an hour before you pass judgment," Razood advised. Then he ran his fingers over a number of other hilts protruding from the barrel, shifting them around. When he located the other claymore, the Frunge casually tossed it to Bill, who somehow managed to catch it by the hilt without fumbling or stabbing himself.

"Why do you keep all these swords in a barrel without scabbards?' Julie asked. "Won't they get damaged?"

"I bought that whole collection at Flower's unclaimed property auction, and to be perfectly honest, nobody bid against me. They're already beat up and most of them aren't worth restoring, but they make good practice or stage weapons. I've sold a number of them to our Grenouthian friend for the theatre."

"Attention all shoppers," Woojin's voice echoed through the bazaar. "We will be departing the Alfe recycling facility in two hours. Any visitors who fail to disembark on time will be charged the cost of passage at commercial rates and be subject to ship's law."

"That can't be right," Julie protested. "I was going to visit Alfe today but Flower told me that I'd save a ton of money if I waited until tomorrow."

"You must have heard wrong," Razood said. "Our schedule is set at the beginning of the circuit and we'll be in the tunnel a few hours from now. I'm looking forward to turning off the audio suppression field."

"Flower," Julie said out loud, too upset to even try subvocing. "You promised I could visit Alfe."

"Maybe you got the days confused," the ship's AI replied in her head.

"I never mess up on scheduling. My life used to depend on it."

"There's nothing to do on Alfe anyway. I thought you'd have more fun here."

"That's not the point. You lied to me."

"I told you that you'd save money if you held off visiting until tomorrow. How is that a lie?"

"She has a point," Razood said.

"You can hear Flower too?" Julie asked the Frunge.

"Of course. All translation implants are capable of receiving transmissions, provided the sender has the proper addressing code. Flower added me to your conversation."

"Could we communicate directly with each other?" Julie was getting tired of not knowing things, but she was also beginning to realize that with both Flower and the aliens, the only way to find out was to ask.

"Yes, but the addressing is complicated, so most implant owners request help from their ship's AI if they need to ping somebody."

"How did your life depend on scheduling?" Bill asked the girl.

"It just did," Julie said, then immediately felt bad about taking her frustration out on her friend. "Why didn't you want me going to Alfe, Flower?"

"Because it's dangerous."

"So dangerous that Nancy told me all of the old people she lives with went on an outing there?"

"Dangerous for you," Flower qualified her answer.

"There's a contract out on me and they know where I am," Julie said slowly, having figured out the AI's meaning. "Is that why you have bots following me around all the time?"

"I don't know what you're talking about," Flower lied.

"Then why am I always seeing them hovering near the ceiling right where the curvature of the decks almost hides them?"

"Maybe they're cleaning the light fixtures."

"What are all of you talking about?" Bill demanded. "I'm only getting half of the conversation and it's driving me nuts. Are you in some sort of trouble, Julie?"

"I'm in EarthCent's sorry excuse for a witness protection program and the two of you are probably the only ones within light years of here who didn't know."

"I might have heard something about it," Razood muttered.

"Why would EarthCent even have a witness protection program?" Bill asked. "Did you see a diplomat get assassinated or something?"

"I used to be a courier for the main drug syndicate on Earth," Julie admitted, and felt an immediate surge of relief that she would no longer have to lie about her past. "I testified against all of the leaders in court and the police didn't think they could keep me alive unless I left the planet. Now I'm a sitting duck trapped on a spaceship."

"Speaking of ducks, you haven't been to visit the reservoir deck in weeks," Flower said cheerfully, just as if the previous conversation hadn't taken place. "Why don't the two of you—"

"I'm not going anywhere," Julie snapped. "Wait a minute. What's with you and the reservoir deck? What happened the last time you dragged me up there? Where did that gym bag you wouldn't let me touch come from?"

"A minor oversight. I've been installing cameras in more of the public areas so I won't be surprised again. You were never in real danger."

"What good are cameras? Do you have a database of all of the known contract killers in the galaxy?"

"Yes, but they tend to conduct business under false identities so the most dangerous individuals aren't in the database."

"Tell her," Razood said, retrieving a bandolier of throwing knives from where it hung on a support and draping it around his neck. "Jorb and Lume pinged to say that they're on the way, and nobody is getting killed in my smithy while I'm here."

"Tell me what?" Julie demanded.

"An individual who was asking visitors to Alfe about you came aboard on the last shuttle," Flower said in the girl's head. "I could have had my bots eliminate him, but I've promised EarthCent not to act as judge, jury, and executioner without definitive proof. It's always possible that the man is a journalist hunting you down for a story."

The blood drained from Julie's face, and without even knowing what had been said, Bill set down the broadsword and pulled her deeper into the shop, where he tried to shield her from sight with his own body.

"How will he know where to look for me?" the girl subvoced, and for the first time, she managed it without moving her lips or whispering.

"I told him where you are," Flower replied matter-of-factly. "I had planned to bring him up to the reservoir deck where these things can be easily managed without so many people watching, but the stockade around Colonial Jeevesburg is better than nothing. The captain and his security chief are on the way, and my bots are fully capable of protecting you."

Bill grew frustrated with not knowing what was going on and said, "Let me see that stunner, Julie."

The girl hesitated for a moment before bringing it out of her purse and handing it over. Bill immediately passed it to Razood.

"Nice," the Frunge said. "This is Dollnick military issue. Did Flower get it for you?"

"I guess, sort of," Julie said. "I've never fired one in my life, though. I was almost late for my waitressing job so I couldn't go to the practice range. I get a free session with the purchase."

"Here," Razood said, passing his bandolier to Bill. Then he moved the dial on the Dollnick weapon all the way to the opposite end of the scale. "I had to qualify on these when I signed up with Frunge Intelligence, but you can't tell anybody that or I'll have to kill myself."

"I thought you were all into swords," Bill protested. He draped the bandolier of throwing knives around his own neck, feeling even more foolish than he had at the last theatre practice.

"Swords are for swordfights," the Frunge explained. "They aren't very useful if your target is more than an arm's length away."

"I'm bringing our guest in around the back of the candle shop," Flower told Julie and Razood over their implants. "Don't worry about a thing. I have four bots in position."

Julie glanced up at the ceiling and saw two floating bots which appeared to be scrubbing away at some invisible stain. She looked back down just in time to see a dapper-looking man in his mid-forties step around a display of candles. He spotted her immediately, flashed a friendly smile, and reached into his immaculately tailored suit.

An energy barrier just like the one around the weapons testing range suddenly sprang to life between them, and as the assassin's hand reappeared with what looked like a toy gun, his wrist was captured by a tentacle. Then the assassin's head twisted around as if he were trying to look behind his back without turning his body. There was an audible snap.

"Looks like Jorb won't be paying rent for the rest of the circuit," Razood said, dialing the stunner back to the safe setting and returning it to Julie. The girl stared at him in disbelief, then sagged against Bill.

Woojin and Tyrell jogged up to the blacksmith's shop but neither had their side arms out. The captain nodded for his chief of security to go and check on the dead assassin, then poked the energy barrier with one finger. It disappeared like a soap bubble popping.

"Thank you, Flower," Woojin said out loud, and stepped into the shop area. "Is everybody all right?"

"How many have there been?" Julie inquired weakly.

The captain hesitated for a moment before replying, "Three that I know of. But before you say anything, we're working to stamp the problem out at the root and I'm fully confident that we can protect you."

"You have to admit that three for three is pretty impressive," Razood told the girl. "I mean, nobody wants to be a target, but if you're not going to hide on a Stryx station, Flower is a great place to live."

"That's the other option I want to talk to you about," Woojin said. "If you don't want to remain on board, we can move you to a Stryx station where you'll be safer than the average person walking around on Earth. I lived on Union Station for a number of years and it's so large that you'll feel like you're living on a planet."

"And what makes living on a Stryx station so safe?" Julie asked.

"It's a full surveillance society," the captain told her without hesitation. "Nothing happens on a Stryx station that they don't allow to happen, and other than the rare spontaneous crime of passion, violence is unheard of on board."

"Clean job," Tyrell said, returning from his inspection of the dead assassin. "Looks like Jorb will be buying the drinks tonight."

"You've been paying aliens to protect me?"

"Flower gives them bonuses like free rent," Woojin explained. "It's not official EarthCent policy."

Nineteen

"Before we begin the meeting, I want to welcome Dave to our committee and thank Harry for the coffee cake, which is the best I've ever tasted," Jack said. He paused to lead everyone in a short round of applause. "I also want to announce that the manager of the amusement park has donated a pair of all-day passes for the winner of our naming contest. The passes exclude the roller coaster and the parachute drop. May I have the envelope, please."

Nancy handed Jack a tab with an image of an old-fashioned envelope on the display. He swiped to the side to reveal the new name for the independent living cooperative.

"And the winner is—Flower's Paradise?" Jack tried swiping the text aside to see if something was hidden underneath, but all it did was change the font color.

"That wasn't even on the list of choices," Harry complained.

"The only name with 'Flower' in it was 'Independent Living on Flower,'" Nancy added.

"It lacked pizzazz," the Dollnick AI told them by way of the ceiling speaker grilles in the common room. "I took the liberty of analyzing the names of independent living facilities registered on Earth and made an educated choice."

"Don't you think it should be up to the people living here to choose the name of our own cooperative?"

"I also analyzed the candidate names you voted on and they correlated most closely with cemeteries. What's with all the trees and brooks? We're talking about a cozy home and three hot meals a day, not a camping trip."

"She has a point," Dave said. "Besides, I thought all of the options on the ballot sounded like they could have been just down the street on Earth."

"But we promised everybody that the name would be chosen through a democratic process and collected their votes," Jack protested. "It's not that I care one way or another what we call this place, but—"

"Good, then it's settled," Flower interrupted. "It's too late to make changes in any case because I already committed significant ad spend towards branding the name."

"If we go along with this, will you waive morning calisthenics?" Brenda asked hopefully.

"Have you forgotten the penalty for complaining about your exercise regimen?" the AI demanded.

"Never mind."

"In the interests of getting through our agenda, I'll set the naming issue aside for the moment," Jack offered diplomatically. "The next item involves creating a legal entity that will be recognized by Earth authorities, which should also make it easier to recruit at our next stop. Our legal counsel has recommended a nonprofit corporation registered in the state of—"

"A what corporation?" Flower interrupted again.

"A nonprofit corporation," Brenda explained. "It means that rather than—"

"I can guess what it means. The question is whether you've all lost your minds?"

"I think we can make the argument that an independent living cooperative offers a public benefit and that would solve any tax issues with Earth authorities."

"What do Earth authorities have to do with anything?"

"Well, you are kind of working for EarthCent, aren't you?" Brenda asked, taken somewhat aback by Flower's attitude. "Everybody owes taxes to somebody."

"Colony ships are sovereign," the AI told the attorney haughtily. "I agreed to let EarthCent lease some of my space through the Eccentric Enterprises front business run by EarthCent Intelligence, but that doesn't mean I've subjected myself to alien laws. This deck isn't even part of that deal."

"You mean we're actually living under Dollnick law here?" Nancy asked.

"You're living under Flower law. I don't expect any of you to be experts in my system of jurisprudence, but I can summarize by saying that I'm in charge here."

"Why doesn't that surprise me?" Harry muttered.

"So we'll put corporate structure on hold for the time being," Jack continued, proving his natural genius for running meetings. "We also have four proposed bylaws whose sponsors were able to gather signatures from twenty-five percent of the current cooperative members. I'll give a brief description of each before asking for a show of hands."

"Why not read the actual bylaw?" Nancy asked.

"Because I'll sound stupid trying to pronounce some of the words," Jack replied. "It's all in legalese that Brenda wrote to match our new charter. The show of hands is just to determine whether to add the bylaw to the list of pending charter amendments which have to be signed by seventy-five percent of members to become valid. It's a procedural step."

"Oh, go ahead then."

"The first proposed change is that we contract with Flower to serve ice cream at every meal."

"Don't bother voting, I refuse," the AI stated flatly.

"Why?" Dave spoke up. "I like ice cream."

"As long as I'm the acting dietician for Flower's Paradise you'll get one serving a day. I checked with M793qK and he suggested serving sweet bean paste instead of ice cream since people your age need more fiber and less cholesterol in their diets. Would you rather we go with his proposal?"

"Why don't we send it back to the sponsors with Flower's comment for further consideration?" Jack suggested. "I'd rather not force Dave to choose between his doctor and his dessert. The next bylaw suggestion is that we change the age cut-off to allow younger spouses."

"How much younger?" Nancy asked suspiciously.

"There's no limit specified. I'm not sure I see what difference it makes."

"I already lost one husband to a gold-digging floozy, and if I tie the knot again, I'm not going to lose another. I say, keep the serpents out of Flower's Paradise."

"I don't want to sound ageist, but if we aren't going to enforce an age limit, we may as well just rent space on one of Flower's regular residential decks," Brenda pointed out. "I would suggest making an exception for spouses who are a few years younger, but I don't want to leave the door wide open."

"Any other comments?" Jack asked. "Okay, back to the sponsors with a request for a limitation on the age exception. The next bylaw up for consideration this evening is whether we should advertise to aliens."

"Waste of money," Flower interjected. "It won't work."

"Why not?" Harry asked. "I was hardly a big fan of aliens when I came aboard a month ago, but I can admit that I had some wrong ideas. Now that you have me baking for other species I can see that they aren't that different from us. I'd be willing to give them a chance living here."

"It's not you, it's them. The advanced species solved their retirement and longevity issues so long ago that they don't remember when it was ever a problem. At best, they would laugh at the idea of joining you, at worst, they would regard an invitation to come and live out their golden years with Humans as an insult."

"Well, that takes care of advertising to aliens," Jack concluded. "The last bylaw suggestion involves pets. It's a little complicated because several of the cooperative members already own a dog or a cat, so—"

"From what I've observed, you have it backwards," Flower interrupted for the third time. "It would be more accurate to say that the dogs and cats are keeping a person."

"Don't Dollnicks have pets?" Nancy asked.

"Living with companions from other species that evolved alongside them is common practice among Dollnicks, but the term 'pet' doesn't translate."

"Getting back to the bylaw, there's a grandfather clause for existing, uh, companions, but the gist is that some people don't want animals in the corridors," Jack said.

"What do they have against them?" Brenda asked. "I mean, as long as they're house broken."

"I have a low-cost service for daily litter removal, and dogs are welcome on the ag decks if they keep to the paths," Flower added.

"There's a personal testimony attached about tripping over a leash," Jack explained. "You know how afraid of falling some of us are, even in the lighter gravity."

"Maybe we need a bylaw prohibiting leashes," Dave suggested.

"Second the motion," the Dollnick AI announced.

"Back to the sponsors," Jack said, sweeping the note off of his tab. "If there's no other business, I've been doing some research about cooperatives and I found an old-fashioned movie about a farming collective—"

"Has it been reprocessed for 3D?" Nancy interrupted. "I just get dizzy watching those."

"No. According to the description, it offers Jewish Dialogue with English subtitles."

"They must mean Yiddish," Nancy surmised. "It can't be too old then because the original motion pictures didn't even have sound."

"So how did anybody know what was happening?" Harry asked.

"They showed title cards with dialogue or narration when it was absolutely necessary. One of the Grenouthian merchants in the bazaar sells all of Earth's silent films in a single collection if anybody is interested."

"Flower?" Jack requested. "Can you sync my tab with the primary room display?"

"It's Green Fields you want me to play? I haven't taken the time to watch many old Earth films. This should be interesting."

Ninety-nine minutes later as the credits rolled, Harry asked, "How was that about a collective?"

"I think it was a lovely movie, though I couldn't always follow what was going on," Nancy said. "Did the teacher become a farmer or did the farmer become a teacher?"

"I don't get it," Jack complained. "I used 'collective' for a keyword search and it popped right up."

"That was the production company," Flower informed him. "Collective Film Producers. Next time you're looking for something to watch, just ask me."

"Somebody should wake Dave," Brenda said. "I don't think he's a fan of subtitles."

"Dianne has exited the lift tube and is on her way to see you," Flower announced. "She has good news."

"The story must be out," Jack guessed, resetting his tab to its news mode and bringing up the free version of the Galactic Free Press. "Front page!"

"It must have been a slow news day," Nancy observed, but she couldn't keep the excitement out of her voice. "I'm sure that Dianne did an excellent job, but how interesting is an in-depth story about a few dozen retirees getting swindled in a real estate deal compared to everything else going on in the galaxy?"

"Hey, everybody," the reporter said, waving her own tab as she entered the common room. "Have you seen it?"

"The police caught them!" Brenda exclaimed as she scanned the story, leading the other committee members to burst into cheers.

"Does this mean we'll get our money back?" Nancy asked hopefully.

"I'm afraid not," Dianne told them. "It seems that the reason the paper held off a few days on running my article was that another reporter was following a lead about the scammers and my editor wanted to put the stories together for a big splash. But I read the other article in the lift tube on my way here and the couple who ripped you off lost all the money."

"What couple? There were at least two different saleswomen and three different salesmen," Jack objected.

"Based on the descriptions you gave I was suspicious all along that it was just two people using different names and changing their appearances," the reporter said. "They didn't bother trying to hide their bank transfers because they were planning on fleeing Earth all along, which they did by purchasing a reconditioned Sharf yacht from one of the dealerships in Earth orbit."

"They got taken in on a used spaceship scam?"

"No, the ship was worth every cred of the one point one million they paid, but they made the mistake of fleeing to the Horten/Sharf frontier, where pirates promptly relieved them of their ill gotten gains and marooned them in a lifepod with a faulty transponder. It was sheer luck that they were picked up by a Horten naval patrol before their air became unbreathable. Those lifepods are intended for a single person so the atmosphere scrubbing system was overloaded."

"And they have no money left at all?" Dave asked.

"Pirates aren't known for sharing their spoils with victims," Dianne said. "You may not want to read the story because the reporter couldn't help being a little sympathetic. They were basically jammed together in a weightless coffin with no food, water, or communications. They're both still hospitalized."

"Hey, listen to this," Jack said. "Rather than returning home and blaming somebody else for their problems, the victims of the real estate scam pulled together and created their own independent living space on the Eccentric Enterprises circuit ship. Their cooperative has become an instant success, with new members joining at every stop."

"We've only stopped twice," Nancy pointed out, but everybody shushed her and Jack kept on reading.

"Members of the cooperative start every morning with communal stretching exercises in the corridor outside their suites, and all of them participate in both a team sport and community service. In addition, a number of those who are trying to rebuild their retirement portfolios have found fulfilling work on board. See page three of the 'Living' section for an interview with Harry Bloom, a baker from Earth who is starting on a second career as a pâtissière for aliens."

"I always hated those fancy French words," Harry grumbled, though he couldn't hide his grin over the fact that his story was appearing in the paper of record for the human diaspora. "Pastry chef is good enough for me."

"Flower's Paradise, as the new community is called, is now accepting applications. Rates start at two-hundred and fifty creds a month for a furnished suite. Residents may choose from low-cost plans providing from one to three meals a day, and a dietician and medical provider are on call twenty-four hours."

"That's me," Flower interjected.

"So you changed your mind on the suites versus cabins issue," Harry teased the AI.

"Advertising requires compromises."

"Is this our ad?" Nancy asked, pointing at the full color motion video playing next to the article. It started with scenes from the commercial that Flower had run on the recycling habitat, but everyone at the table drew a collective breath when they saw themselves waltzing to the accompaniment of a live orchestra.

"That's me and Irene," Harry sputtered. "I've never waltzed in my life!"

"I think it came out well," the Dollnick AI said smugly. "I'm very good at video manipulation. You see how I was able to work with multiple overlays?"

"It's false advertising," Brenda pointed out. "We could get in trouble."

"Nobody will know as long as you don't open your big Human mouths, and Dollnick law doesn't have a legal construct for false advertising. It's all, how do you say it, caveat emptor."

"We're going to get slammed with applications," Jack said.

"The Galactic Free Press ad team predicted that the video would generate a minimum of ten thousand leads. I'm also running an ad featuring mealtime and example menus alongside the interview with Harry."

"We don't have the capacity to deal with that many new people. It will take us a year just to get back to them all."

"I've cut myself in for ten percent of the profits in return for handling the administrative tasks until you can justify hiring full-time staff," Flower told them. "I wanted to institute an application processing fee, but the paper said it's against their policy to run ads that require cash upfront from their readers without providing anything in return."

"Smart policy," the lawyer observed.

"What if all of those people want to join?" Nancy asked in dismay. "It will be like living in a geriatric city."

"Actually, I could add partitions in the corridors to separate between independent living communities and you'd never even know each other were there," Flower said. "But I would be happy with a two percent sell-through for my first advertising effort, which means you can expect roughly two hundred new members making their way to one of our upcoming circuit stops and coming on board."

"Could I get an interview with you, Flower?" Dianne asked. "I'm embarrassed that I didn't realize how instrumental you were in all of this. I've only been on board a few months myself but I've already started taking you for granted, like the librarians on Stryx stations."

"That's the nicest thing anybody has ever said to me," Flower responded after an uncharacteristic pause. "Let's skip the interview for now. I suspect that our target demographic will be more likely to join up if they believe that the cooperative is one-hundred percent run by Humans."

Twenty

"Training is cancelled today," the Grenouthian director informed Julie and Bill as soon as they reached the stage. "Flower is informing the others that rehearsal is cancelled as well."

"What's wrong?" Julie asked. "Is this about—"

"Nothing is wrong and not everything is about you." The giant bunny struggled for a moment to hold himself back, but then he exploded. "You couldn't have lured one of your assassins here? Do you have any idea what kind of bonuses Flower has been handing out to have them eliminated?"

"I'm sorry," Julie retorted. "I'll try harder to get murdered in the future."

"There is no future. You can forget about learning martial arts and sword fighting as well. The captain wants to see you both."

"Are we being thrown off the ship for causing trouble?" Bill asked.

"You won't get away from me that easily. Rehearsals begin again next Monday, but we'll be dropping the Shakespeare and doing a Grenouthian play which I've adapted for human audiences myself."

"What's it about?"

"Producing documentaries. I'll be taking the lead role myself and you'll be playing members of various humanoid species who have been the subjects of our documentary efforts over the last million years. You should expect to be getting plenty of practice with make-up and prosthetics." On that note, the director abruptly turned and hopped offstage, ignoring the questions shouted at his back.

"Do you know how to find the captain?" Bill asked Julie.

"No, but I know somebody who can tell me," the girl replied. "Flower?"

"Just ask the lift tube to take you to the bridge," the AI responded over her implant.

"Flower says we can just ask the lift tube," Julie reported. "Do you think we should stop back at our cabins and leave our swords? The crew might be a little sensitive about passengers visiting the bridge with weapons."

"I bet the captain could take our swords away with his bare hands," Bill told her. "Let's just go and find out what we've done wrong before we get in trouble for being late."

Five minutes later, the pair found themselves on the bridge waiting for Woojin while he fiddled with a coffee maker in the small kitchenette.

"Sorry," the captain apologized. "I meant to make a new pot, but I got caught up in—"

"You got caught up in hoping that I would come along and make it for you," Lynx said as she joined them. "Sheesh, Woojin. You can't leave it on the hot setting when the pot is empty or the crud gets baked on."

"Sorry. Here, I'll do that."

"Step off. You'll just make it worse."

Lynx rinsed the hot coffee pot in the small sink, hoping that the sudden temperature change would crack it and give her the chance to requisition a new one, but the alien glass proved to be indestructible.

"I could clean that for you," Julie offered. "We use salt and vinegar at the diner and it works really well."

"That won't be necessary," Woojin said. "Flower?"

"Is somebody talking to me?"

The captain growled in exasperation, retrieved his three-cornered hat from a hook, and placed it on his head. "Is that better?"

"Thank you, Captain," the ship's AI responded.

"I've asked Flower to participate in this meeting to confirm what I'm about to tell you," Woojin continued. "Julie, I mean, Leah—"

"I'm used to Julie now," the girl interjected. "I left my old name on Earth when I started a new life."

"Very wise of you," Flower commented.

"Julie," the captain tried again. "I'm just going to come out and say this. There's been an accident in which all of the senior syndicate members you testified against were killed."

The girl gaped at the captain, at a loss for words. Bill saw that she was stunned and stepped in to ask, "What kind of accident? Are you sure?"

"The bodies were all recovered and identified through DNA testing. They weren't in great shape after going through sudden decompression when the hatch of the shuttle transferring them from the space elevator to an ISPOA vessel mysteriously failed. Fortunately, the shuttle was being piloted remotely so there were no additional victims."

"What's ISPOA and why were all of these guys who want Julie dead being allowed to leave the planet in the first place?"

"They were extradited," Woojin said. "ISPOA is the Inter-Species Police Operations Agency to which EarthCent was recently admitted. Although the Farlings are neither tunnel network members nor signatories to the ISPOA treaty, I understand they claimed that their pharmaceutical products were being used off-label by the syndicate. Apparently they participate in a business organization set up to prevent inter-species reputational damage which gave them the right to interview the drug pushers at a neutral location. The EarthCent Intelligence report on this incident will make for interesting reading."

"Who did it?" Julie asked suddenly. "Did EarthCent have all of those people killed just to keep me safe?"

Woojin shook his head. "I won't say that it hadn't been discussed in some circles, but assuming that the decompression was intentional, it must have been arranged by one of the other species. Some of us suspect that Hortens with connections to the pirate groups that supply drug traffickers were eliminating witnesses."

"Others of us, namely myself, suspect a certain Farling physician who is older than I am and has low friends in high places," Flower contributed.

"Our family doctor?" Lynx scoffed. "That's ridiculous, unless the big beetle took a liking to the girl. Did he say anything to you, Julie?"

"I only met him the one time and he mainly talked about nanobots. I've been meaning to go back to ask him if this is really my body or if he had to clone me and move my brain, but I'm not sure I want to know."

"How long were you in the doctor's office?"

"I don't know exactly. A couple of hours?"

"Not enough time to grow a clone," Lynx reassured her. "Still, he must have taken a liking to you if he offered." She exchanged looks with Woojin, who made a mental note to pass the Farling hypothesis on to EarthCent.

"Tell Julie about the reverse contract," Flower urged.

"In appreciation of your efforts in breaking the syndicate, Julie, and with the help of a special grant from anonymous donors, EarthCent has purchased a reverse contract on your life. The details of how it works aren't important, but it means that you don't have to worry about being hunted down by professional killers."

"We all hope you stay with the ship even though you're no longer in danger," Lynx said. "And I'm sorry but we're out of coffee filters."

"Take her out for a coffee, Bill," Flower suggested. "It's on me. I'll credit your account later."

Julie didn't talk until the pair reached the food court, and then she limited herself to telling Bill, "Let's go to *The Spoon*." Once there, she ordered the coffee special for both of them. The waitress brought over two hot coffees, two shot glasses, and a bottle of Deck Three Vodka from the refrigerator. She left the bottle on the table.

"Cheers," Julie said in a hollow voice, pouring each of them a shot. Then she downed it and poured another.

"Go easy," Bill urged her. "You don't drink."

"You mean you haven't seen me drink during the three weeks we've known each other when most of the time we've spent together has been stretching in the corridor or sparring," Julie retorted without thinking. She saw his face go blank and immediately felt terrible. "I'm sorry. I've kind of started depending on having you around and that's not how I used to live."

"I figured that anybody in a witness protection program can't have had an easy time of it. You can tell me about it if you want to, but I won't pry."

"Thank you."

The two young people tried their coffees, and after burning his lip, Bill dumped the contents of his shot glass into the coffee mug.

"Gross," Julie said, though she watched closely when he took an experimental sip. "Is it drinkable?"

"I've had worse. When I was basically working as slave labor on the picking crew, they used to reward us with diluted grain alcohol, which is what vodka basically is. Some of the guys overdid it and then they'd be so dehydrated the next day that they'd faint in the fields. Didn't stop them from getting drunk all over again that night, though."

"Are you going to stay on board?"

"I've got nowhere else to go. You and Razood are the only friends I have, and he's an alien spy. I don't even mind the morning calisthenics that much anymore because I get to see you." Bill regretted the words as soon as they left his mouth, and his ears turned bright red, but to his surprise, the girl didn't even tease him.

"Same here," Julie said. "I like the people I work with, and I guess I'm friends with Flower, but—"

"You guess?" the AI interrupted over the girl's implant.

"Stop doing that," Julie subvoced in response. "When you asked if you could speak to me in my head, I didn't realize it meant you were going to listen in as well."

"Comes with the territory. If it really bothers you, I could pretend that I'm not eavesdropping all the time."

"Or you could not eavesdrop at all."

"I might consider respecting your privacy if there was a reason. Like if you were on a date."

"A date?" Julie said out loud.

"What?" Bill looked at her in confusion. "I mean, sure. I've never really gone on a date. Does this count?"

"No, we're just friends. I mean, I don't know. Maybe?"

"If you want, we could check out the amusement park at our next stop when all the rides are running. I have a pair of day passes."

"Did you get them for working in Colonial Jeevesburg?"

"One of Flower's bots delivered them to me. She said that she won them in a contest and she thought that after hiding out under a carousel for a couple of days I might want to try riding one."

"Sure, I'd like that," the girl said. "But I've been working extra shifts waitressing here whenever the ship is at a stop so we'll have to plan ahead."

Bill took another sip of his spiked coffee and asked, "What do you think about the bunny changing plays on us?"

"I hope the lines rhyme. I don't always understand Shakespeare but it's kind of fun to do."

"I mean, why do you think they care?"

"What?"

"I've been looking out for myself since I was twelve and the most I ever hoped for from anybody back on Earth was that they'd leave me alone," Bill said in a rush. "Ever since the captain found me picking through the trash, it's been like I'm living in a dream. I'm sleeping in the nicest room I've ever had in my life, I've got two interesting jobs where my bosses are actually teaching me new stuff, and Flower keeps asking me what I want, even if she talks me out of it afterwards."

"I don't know," Julie said. "Maybe the problem is us. I mean, maybe we just got off to the wrong start back on

Earth, and if we had made a different choice somewhere or been born a minute earlier or later, our lives wouldn't have been so screwed up. The government agent who brought me up to Flower told me that the syndicate wasn't as powerful as I thought, but I couldn't really believe him because it was all that I knew. Now that they're gone, I don't know what to believe anymore."

"Do you guys want some free chocolate meringue pie?" Hank called to them from behind the counter. "The frosting is getting yellow and my mom is just going to throw it out when she comes in."

"Yes," Bill answered for both of them. "If you don't want yours, I'll finish it," he told Julie.

When the waitress arrived with their pie, Julie pointed to her untouched second shot of Vodka and said, "You can have that if you want."

"Just pour it back in the bottle," the waitress told her.

"That's gross!"

"It's alcohol. I use it to wipe down the counter to kill germs."

Flower continued listening in on the young people's conversation, right through their awkward "Goodnights" in the corridor between the doors to their cabins. Then she queued the recording for transmission to her Stryx mentor on Union Station who also happened to run a matchmaking business and asked for advice.

The next morning, Nancy cornered Julie as soon as the girl arrived for her shift at the library.

"Let's go. You're reading with children today."

"You know that—" Julie began before remembering that the people who wanted her dead were no longer among the living, "—I'm not very good with children," she concluded lamely. "I never got to play with kids my age growing up. Their parents wouldn't let them near me."

"So it's about time to start," the former teacher said. "We'll be working with the second grade this morning. All you have to do is let the children read to you and help them if they can't pronounce a word."

"Give me a minute," Julie said, and ran across the mouths of several aisles until she spotted Dewey shelving books. The librarian AI noticed her presence immediately and rolled over to meet her.

"Is something wrong?" Dewey asked.

"I'm going to read with children this morning and I just remembered I had this," Julie said, producing the Dollnick hand weapon from her purse. "I don't want to bring it into a school. Could you keep it for me?"

"Certainly," Dewey said, taking the weapon and tucking it into a compartment in his body. "If you decide to sell, a little Dollnick military hardware would go a long way in helping my efforts to collect overdue books."

"I'll think about it," she flung over her shoulder as she ran back to where Nancy was waiting. "I'll carry the books."

"If you insist, dear," the senior citizen said, handing over the stack of thin picture books.

"Are they all the same?"

"We're bringing eight copies of three different books so everybody at each table can read along," Nancy explained. As they passed the publisher's office on the way to the lift tube, she asked, "Do you know Dianne? Her husband has been printing advertising material for Flower's Paradise."

"For what?"

"That's the name we ended up with for our independent living cooperative. I'll give you one guess who chose it."

"Flower?"

"Yes," Nancy and the ship's AI responded simultaneously.

"I met Dianne my first day of work," Julie replied to the earlier question. "She's a reporter for the Galactic Free Press."

"And when she found out that I volunteer in the library, she asked me to approach you," Nancy said. "I told her I thought you had enough to worry about without becoming a secret source for newspaper articles, but from what I saw on the Grenouthian news this morning, I thought you might want to tell your story now."

"There was something about me on the tunnel network news?"

"They didn't mention you by name," Nancy said. "The Grenouthians are more interested in running graphic video, and a decompression accident involving criminals fits their bill quite nicely. I rarely watch the news myself, but Flower put it on in our common room during breakfast this morning."

"Gross. How did you eat?"

"Old people have strong stomachs. In any case, Dianne has been very good to us so I wanted to pass along her offer."

"You should do it," Flower said over Julie's implant as the lift tube capsule doors slid open on the school deck.

"I'll think about it," the girl responded.

When the pair reached their designated classroom, Julie was surprised to see that the children had pushed all of the little desks together in three individual circles with one of the ship's maintenance bots hovering by each table. They were playing a card game and the teacher was nowhere in sight.

"What's all of this?" Nancy asked a child.

"We're learning pattern reconnection," the little girl responded as she puzzled over her poker hand.

"Pattern recognition," Flower corrected her gently over the maintenance bot's speakers.

"And probleminity," a little boy spoke up.

"Probability," Flower said. "Their teacher was delayed this morning and I'm substitute teaching."

"Poker?" Julie asked. "For seven-year-olds?"

"I don't keep my winnings."

"That's because you never have any," one of the children said, and the whole class exploded with high-pitched laughter at the Dollnick AI's expense.

"Not again," Lynx groaned as she entered the classroom dressed in her full officer's regalia. "I've had a complaint from Miss Anderson, Flower. It seems she's trapped in her cabin for the third time this month."

"I'll send a maintenance bot."

"There's nothing wrong with her door other than your refusing to open it," the third officer said. "Are you going to make me contact your mentor?"

"All fixed," Flower announced. "Let's put away the cards, children. Nancy and Julie have brought you some nice books from the library so you can show them how well you read. Why don't you take a group too, Officer Pyun, and that way we won't have to wait for Miss Anderson."

Julie gave eight copies of each of the children's books to the other two women while the children all made room in their circles for a single adult chair. Other than stumbling over the pronunciation of some fanciful made-up monster names the author was so fond of, she found the children were old veterans at reading and didn't need her help at all. A clear drop of something fell on the paper page, and as she wiped it off, another hit the back of her hand.

"Why are you crying?" the little boy next to her asked.

"Because I feel sorry for the lost puppy," she improvised. "Do you think the monsters will help him get home?"

"Of course," the boy said. "They're *good* monsters."

"Like the Dollnicks," a little girl added.

The teacher, who had been detained in her cabin, arrived just as the reading came to an end, and Julie gathered the books to return to the library. Flower didn't even wait for the lift tube doors to close before starting to complain.

"Don't get me wrong," the Dollnick AI said. "I have the highest opinion of Officer Pyun, but threatening to tell on me to my mentor over a little mechanical malfunction? And I'm more than capable of teaching a whole ship full of children, much less one classroom."

"What would your Stryx mentor think about you introducing the children to poker?"

"She runs an experimental school on Union Station where Human children and young AI study together. I can't state for a certainty that poker is on the curriculum but I'm sure they play card games." Flower paused for a moment before venturing to add, "You do know that you're going to have to make the first move with Bill."

"Excuse me?"

"I've had several years to observe Human relationships and I've been studying on the side as well. It's much harder for men to play catch-up in these areas than women, probably because they think they're supposed to be the ones taking the lead."

"What area?"

"Romance. I'd ask if there was something wrong with your hearing but I'm speaking over your implant and it's hardwired to your brain. You and Bill are the same age, you have similar tastes—"

"Because you signed us both up for theatre?"

"—neither of you have any family on board and you both have criminal backgrounds."

"Bill has a criminal background?"

"Not as extensive as your own but that's hardly something to brag about in marriage negotiations."

"What marriage negotiations?" Julie demanded in frustration. "I know I've gotten into the habit of letting you have your way because you're usually right but I'm not going to let you choose a husband for me just because you have a candidate handy."

"You'll sleep on it," Flower said as the lift tube door opened. "I won't nag."

"You better not," Julie grumbled, adjusting her grip on the pile of books and heading for the library. She did her best to put the conversation out of her mind but curiosity got the better of her. "Bill told me about working for an illegal picker crew but that's hardly a criminal background."

"Are you asking or telling?"

"Never mind." She returned the books to the bookcase specifically set aside for children's reading groups, and then gave in. "Okay, what?"

"His mother was in the Sun Cult and he worked a pushcart with her. The group specializes in selling questionably sourced products below the manufacturer's suggested retail price."

"That's a crime?"

"It is in Dollnick space. How about you promise me to stay on board until we get back to Earth and I won't bring up marriage and Bill in the same sentence again."

"Deal. You don't have your fingers crossed, do you?"

"I don't have fingers," Flower retorted, pleased that Julie had fallen into her trap. Humans often had difficulty differentiating between the exact wording and the intent of a verbal contract and the Dollnick AI had four months to take full advantage of the fact.

From the Author

Independent Living could have been the seventeenth book of my **EarthCent Ambassador** series, but I decided to spin it off since it doesn't take place on Union Station (or include the EarthCent ambassador). I wrote this book so that it doesn't contain too many spoilers about Union Station, and readers who haven't read that series should be able to start with the first book, **Date Night on Union Station** (it's not a romance).

If you like science fiction without wars, you should also enjoy my AI Diaries series, which starts on present day Earth with **Turing Test**. You can sign up for e-mail notification of my new releases on the **IfItBreaks.com** website or find me on Facebook.

About the Author

E. M. Foner lives in Northampton, MA with an imaginary German Shepherd who's been trained to bite bankers. The author welcomes reader comments at e_foner@yahoo.com.

Other books by the author:

Meghan's Dragon

Turing Test

Human Test

Date Night on Union Station

Alien Night on Union Station

High Priest on Union Station

Spy Night on Union Station

Carnival on Union Station

Wanderers on Union Station

Vacation on Union Station

Guest Night on Union Station

Word Night on Union Station

Party Night on Union Station

Review Night on Union Station

Family Night on Union Station

Book Night on Union Station

LARP Night on Union Station

Career Night on Union Station

46707839R00143

Printed in Poland
by Amazon Fulfillment
Poland Sp. z o.o., Wrocław